Stranded ;

MW01148003

Crash and Burn
Rachel Lacey

Henderson County Public Library

COPYRIGHT

This book is licensed to you for your personal enjoyment only.

This is a work of fiction. Names, characters, places, and incidents are either products of the writer's imagination or are used fictitiously and are not to be construed as real. Any resemblance to actual events, locales, organizations, or persons, living or dead, is entirely coincidental.

Crash and Burn
Copyright © 2017 by Rachel Lacey
ISBN: 978-1975884413
Cover design by Letitia Hasser, Romantic Book Affairs

ALL RIGHTS RESERVED.
No part of this work may be used, reproduced, or transmitted in any form or by any means, electronic or mechanical, without prior permission in writing from the publisher, except in the case of brief quotations embodied in critical articles or reviews.

NYLA Publishing
350 7th Avenue, Suite 2003, NY 10001, New York.
http://www.nyliterary.com

Henderson County Public Library

DEDICATION:

This book is dedicated to the real-life heroes of Pilots n Paws who go above and beyond to provide countless rescue pets a second chance.

CHAPTER ONE

ISABEL Delgado took one look at the silver-paneled airplane in front of her and shook her head. Nope. No friggin' way. Her fingers tightened around the red nylon leash in her right hand. Somehow, when she'd decided to accompany Maya the Husky on her freedom flight from the Orange County Animal Shelter to the rescue awaiting her in Oregon, she'd failed to take into consideration the size—or lack thereof—of the plane they'd be flying on.

"Ms. Delgado?"

Isa gulped a breath and focused on the man who'd just stepped out of the tiny plane. He watched her through mirrored sunglasses, his expression intense. A black T-shirt was stretched across his muscular chest, well-worn jeans hugged his narrow hips, and well, now her heart was pounding for an entirely different reason. When Silicon Valley CEO Nathaniel Peters had offered to fly them on the first leg of their journey, she hadn't expected him to be so young...or hot.

"You can call me Isa," she said, extending a hand.

"Nate." He took her hand and gave it a quick, firm shake. "And this must be Maya."

Isa glanced down at the dog. Maya stood, blue eyes alert, muscles tensed, ready to bolt at the slightest provocation. There was a reason the shelter workers called her Houdini, the same reason Isa was accompanying her on her rescue flight with Pilots for Pets instead of just handing her over to Nate: Maya was a serious flight risk.

"Ready?" Nate asked.

Isa looked again at the little silver plane behind him. Her palms dampened, and a sick feeling gripped the pit of her stomach. "Ah—how safe is that plane?"

"The Cirrus SR22 is one of the safest personal aircraft out there," Nate said, his deep voice betraying a hint of annoyance.

"And you've been flying awhile?"

"Fifteen years." He turned toward the plane. "We'd better get a move on."

"Okay," she answered, but her voice had drifted away to nothing, and her feet refused to budge.

"Is there a problem?"

She cleared her throat. "I wasn't expecting it to be so...small."

"Look, if you're having second thoughts, I can take the dog myself."

Isa's fingers tightened around the leash. Undoubtedly, this wasn't the *best* way to overcome her fear of flying, but if she got the promotion she'd just applied for at work, she'd have to fly all over the country to visit client sites, and besides, Maya really did need an escort. Isa had been visiting and walking her at the shelter for months. Maya trusted her.

"No, I'm coming." She lifted her overnight bag from the tarmac and walked toward Nate and his plane. Maya, whether sensing Isa's fear or acting on her own misgivings, wrenched her head, attempting to slip out of her collar and make a run for it. Isa stepped backward to keep slack on the leash, preventing the dog from escaping. "Not on my watch," she told Maya. "Come on. You're going to love Oregon when we get there. Lots of snow. Maybe your new family will even get you a little sled to pull."

Nate gestured toward the plane. "You'll ride beside me. She can have the backseat."

Isa walked around to the passenger door, which was directly above the plane's shiny silver wing. "How do I get in?"

"Just step right onto the mat," Nate said, indicating a black mat laid across the wing. "Need a hand?"

"No, thanks." She patted the mat, and Maya hopped up. Once the dog had climbed inside the plane, Isa followed her, gawking as she settled into her seat. It was almost like the interior of a fancy car—two plush leather seats in front and three in the back. The glaring difference was the huge instrument panel in front of her.

Nate swung her door shut and latched it, then walked around the plane. He stowed their bags behind the rear seat and climbed in beside her. "Nervous flier?"

3

She loosened her white-knuckled grip on the armrests. "Terrified, to be perfectly honest, but I promised myself I was going to overcome my fear of flying today, and once I decide to do something, there's no going back."

He nodded. "Just so you know, this is going to feel a lot different from a commercial flight. The Cirrus moves with every gust of wind."

Sweat prickled under Isa's arms. "Okay."

"We'll be flying over the Sierra Nevadas today. Should be a pretty ride," Nate commented as he began messing with the controls in front of him. "It's going to be loud in here once I start the engine. You can go ahead and put on the headset in front of you."

She reached forward and put on the headset as the engine roared to life. Her heart was whirling as fast as the propeller in front of them. Nate spoke to air traffic control as the rumble of the propeller grew louder. Its blades blurred before her eyes.

From the backseat, Maya whined. Isa twisted around to check on her, stroking behind her ears the way Maya preferred. Rubbing the dog seemed to have a calming effect on both of them, so Isa concentrated on Maya, petting and comforting her as the plane began to roll forward. And then…they were hurtling down the runway.

Isa leaned back in her seat and squeezed her eyes shut. She felt the moment when they left the asphalt. The jostling bump of the wheels ceased, and her stomach performed a barrel roll as they soared upward. The sensation was dizzying and disorienting.

"Great view of the coast if you want to open

4

your eyes," Nate commented a minute or so later, his voice coming in loud and clear through the headset she wore.

Isa forced herself to peek, and *whoa*, they were high up. And yeah, the glittering California coastline below was absolutely stunning. But they were so high up...

"Should take us about three hours to reach Reno," Nate said.

She nodded, gulping for air. Her arms had started to tingle, and she couldn't stop the dizzying flop of her stomach, like she'd swallowed a live fish and it was flailing around inside her, trying to escape. Maya, on the contrary, had settled down on the backseat, head between her front paws, as if she flew all the time.

No big deal.

Right. Isa sucked in another breath, willing herself to calm down. The plane climbed, banked right, and climbed some more. From time to time, Nate commented on the weather or the terrain beneath them, but she was too scared to look. After a half hour or so, though, she had relaxed enough that she was able to speak without fear of losing her lunch.

"So you do this for fun, huh?" She looked at Nate.

He still wore his mirrored shades, hiding the color of his eyes. His hair was a rich espresso brown, his skin tanned as though he spent plenty of time outdoors. "Started flying when I was eighteen. Love the adrenaline rush, the freedom. I spend sixty to eighty hours a week in the office. This is my escape."

She risked a glance at the mountainous

5

landscape below and immediately wished she hadn't. The plane seemed to catch a dip in the air, or maybe it was just Isa's stomach lurching as she took in the craggy peaks beneath them. "I prefer the beach."

"Probably more dangerous than flying, all things considered," he said. "Sharks, rip currents…"

"I never said I went in the water." Actually, she loved to swim. Flying was her only real phobia, and she was *this* close to overcoming it too.

He was silent for a moment, fiddling with the controls. "There's smoke ahead from a wildfire. I'm going to detour to the east."

Nate was a hard guy to read. All business. She wondered if he ever let loose or even cracked a smile. He didn't come across as stuffy or rude, though, and it had to say something about his character that he donated his time to help fly rescue pets out of shelters. After he dropped Isa and Maya off in Reno, they would be boarding a second flight with another pilot, who was taking them to Portland.

It promised to be an exhausting day, but seeing Maya safely to her new foster family ought to be a good enough reward. That, and conquering her fear of flying. Since Nate didn't seem to be much of a conversationalist, Isa pulled out her Kindle and settled back in her seat to read. She made sure to pick a happy, fluffy romance with absolutely no scary parts. Flying in a tin can over the Sierra Nevadas while a wildfire raged below was scary enough on its own.

She zoned out as the characters in her book fought their attraction for each other while the hero taught the heroine how to make pizza from scratch. It was messy and surprisingly sexy. A loud pop brought her back to reality sometime later. She looked up from her Kindle just as an alarm began to sound in the instrument panel in front of her. Nate swore. And was it her imagination, or did the engine sound funny all of a sudden?

"Don't panic," Nate said as he adjusted one of the controls.

Don't panic? Isa gripped the armrests. This was so much more stress than she'd needed for her first-ever flight. She was an idiot not to have booked herself a quick trip to San Francisco or Las Vegas—someplace fun with a big, comfy commercial jet to get her there—because this...this was terrifying.

"What's happening?" she asked as a shudder ran through the plane. Fear clutched her stomach like an icy fist.

"Figuring that out right now," he said, continuing to read various gauges and screens in front of him.

The engine coughed, spluttered, and stopped. What? No. No way. This was not happening! The sudden silence was deafening. Her worst nightmare was coming true...

Nate twisted a key to his left, and the engine roared back to life.

Oh, thank God.

She sucked in a breath as relief swept through her system. With another cough, the engine silenced again. And this time it stayed off. The propeller in front of them twisted to a stop, along with Isa's heart.

"*Dios mío,*" she whispered, clutching her chest. They were going to crash in the mountains in the

7

middle of a forest fire. This was it. She was done for.

"We've had some kind of mechanical failure, possibly a faulty intake valve," Nate said, his voice still irrationally calm. "The engine's seized up. Hang tight." He pushed a button in front of him and started speaking into the radio. When she heard him say "Mayday," something inside her snapped.

Isa prayed quietly, clinging to her seat. They glided along, plunging into a bank of clouds, with nothing but the eerie whistling of the wind outside her window to remind her that they'd lost power.

They were going down.

She was only twenty-seven years old. She'd never even been in love. She wanted to get married and have babies…and *oh God…*

This was not how she was going to die. No, no, no!

The plane glided lower, bursting out of the clouds into clear air. Isa blinked. Off in the distance, flames glowed red through the trees. Below them, craggy mountains loomed, promising a swift, brutal end to their flight.

Nate was still on the radio, calling in their location as he tried again to restart the engine. He guided them over the rocky peaks below toward mossy green treetops in the distance.

"She's equipped with a 'chute if it comes to that," he said.

"A what?" Isa's brain was misfiring, trying to reconcile this eerily calm, quiet descent with the disaster waiting at the end.

"A parachute. I'm looking for a soft spot to set her down."

Set her down? As in, *not die?*

But Isa didn't see anything that looked like a "soft spot." She saw only rocks, and trees, and more rocks... She squeezed her eyes shut and sent up another silent prayer.

"I'm going to put us in the lake," Nate said a few moments later.

She opened her eyes. A lake twinkled sapphire blue up ahead. It looked as good a place as any to crash-land, but it was so far away. Could they really glide that far?

"Brace yourself, Isa. I'm going to pull the 'chute. Grab ahold of your seat belt."

She did as he said, gripping the straps that crossed her chest. With his right hand, Nate reached back and pushed Maya into the foot of the backseat area. He held her down while, with his left hand, he reached up and pulled a red handle overhead.

A horrific boom reverberated through the airplane as it jerked as though it had just slammed into something solid. Isa screamed. The plane pitched nose down toward the ground, her head slammed into the window beside her, and everything went black.

CHAPTER TWO

NATE twisted in his seat to check on his passengers. Isa sat beside him, clutching her head, while Maya scrambled to her feet behind them. For a few hair-raising seconds after he pulled the parachute, they had dangled nose down beneath it, but now the plane had leveled out and was drifting toward the lake ahead just as he had planned.

"You okay?" he asked Isa.

She nodded, her expression dazed and glassy, rubbing at a red lump on her temple. They had maybe a minute until impact. The Cirrus wouldn't float for long, so he needed to make the most of every second they had to spare before then. He sure hoped Isa—and Maya—were up for a swim, because they were fresh out of alternatives.

He unfastened his seat belt and crawled in

back, lowering the seat to retrieve his and Isa's overnight bags. If she and the dog were able to swim unassisted, he'd try to get the bags to shore. Who knew how long they'd have to wait for rescue? The provisions inside might be the difference between life and death.

"Can you swim?" he asked Isa as he shoved the plane's first aid kit inside his duffel bag.

"Yes," she answered faintly.

"Can she?" he asked, pointing to the dog.

"I d-don't know." Isa's teeth were chattering. She was going into shock, and her timing couldn't be worse.

He crawled back into the front seat with their bags and refastened his seat belt. "Take off your headset and your shoes."

She stared at him blankly for a moment, then removed her headset and slid off her sneakers. He kicked off his loafers and tied both pairs of shoes to his bag. They'd swim better this way.

"I'm going to open the doors now," he told her. The lake glistened maybe fifty feet below. They had only seconds left. He unlatched his door and swung it up, then reached over Isa and did the same to hers. Wind rushed through the interior of the plane, and Isa screamed.

"Why did you do that?" She clutched frantically at the straps of her seat belt.

"When we hit that lake, we're going to need to get out fast. When I say go, you're going to unclip your seat belt, climb out on the wing, and jump."

"Oh God...oh God." She closed her eyes, continuing to mutter under her breath.

11

And then, with a jolt, they smacked into the lake. Water sprayed around them, soaking the interior of the plane. Isa screamed again, throwing her hands up in front of her face. The plane lurched left, then forward before finally coming to a rest.

Immediately, he unclipped both of their seat belts. The Cirrus currently bobbed on the lake's surface, but it wouldn't float for long, especially not once the parachute began to drag them down. "It's go time, Isa. Just scoot out on the wing and start swimming toward shore. I'll take care of Maya."

"Wh-what?" She looked at him, her eyes unfocused.

Dammit. "You've got to swim."

He put on her backpack and slung his duffel bag over top of it. The water was up to their ankles now and rising fast. It was ice cold, and they had a good five-hundred-yard swim to shore. He sure as hell hoped she was up for it. "Are you ready?"

"Ready," she whispered.

"Now, Isa. Jump."

She sat there, eyes wide, visibly trembling, and his heart clenched. He really didn't want to drag her out of her seat, but they needed to go, *now*. The plane began to list to one side.

"Go," he said softly as water continued to pour into the cabin. Thirty seconds, and his beloved Cirrus would be gone.

Isa crawled onto the wing and flopped sideways into the lake, disappearing below the surface. Fear bolted through him, but a moment later, she was up and swimming.

Nate turned his attention to the dog, who was

whining and thrashing around in the rapidly filling rear of the plane. He slid his fingers beneath her collar and guided her to the door. Here's hoping Huskies could swim...

Maya bobbed into the lake and began to paddle.

Heaving a breath of relief, Nate pushed himself out of the plane and kicked off in the direction Isa had gone. Behind him, with an ominous sucking sound, the Cirrus slipped beneath the surface. Gone.

Seven years and over one thousand hours of flight time together—possibly the longest relationship he'd ever had. But he and his passengers were alive. If they made it out of this mess, he could buy himself a new plane. He adjusted the bags on his back and swam after Isa and Maya.

"Oh no," Isa moaned as he drew even with her.

"What's wrong?"

"Maya!" she cried.

The dog had left them in her wake, paddling swiftly toward shore with her red leash trailing behind her in the water.

"It's okay. She looks like a strong swimmer."

"But she's Houdini! We'll never see her again." Isa kicked with renewed vigor. The cold water seemed to have brought her back to her senses, and she swam ahead of him with more strength and speed than he had expected.

Still, it was a long ten minutes before they reached the shore. Nate was winded and shivering by the time he followed Isa onto the rocky shoreline.

Her lips were purple and shaking, her cocoa eyes wide, her dark hair plastered to her head, and she looked so fucking beautiful, he almost pulled her into his arms and kissed her because they were *alive*.

"We survived," she whispered.

"Fucking right, we did."

She flung her arms around him. For a moment, he just stood there, caught off guard by her impulsiveness, before hugging her back. Her whole body trembled against his—adrenaline, or cold. Probably both.

"We lost Maya," she said against his neck, a tremor in her voice.

"What are you talking about?" He pointed toward the edge of the tree line, where the dog sat watching. "She's right there."

"Oh!" Isa released him and crouched, extending her arms toward the dog. "Maya, you beautiful thing. I'm so glad to see you."

Maya walked toward her cautiously, wet and bedraggled but otherwise none the worse for wear. She pressed her head into Isa's lap.

"I can't believe it. At the shelter, she was always trying to escape." She stroked the dog behind her ears.

"Maybe she just didn't like being in a cage," he said.

"Maybe. So how long do you think it will be before they send out a search party for us?"

He cringed inwardly at the hopeful expression on her face. "I'm not sure my distress call went through. If it didn't, it'll take a few hours for them to realize we haven't arrived in Reno. They might be

14

able to send out search and rescue for us today, but they won't have many hours of daylight left. I think we should plan on spending at least one night here."

"At *least* one night?" Isa's pretty face paled.

"I deviated from our flight plan to skirt the forest fire. They may not know where to look." He paused, glancing at the black smoke visible in the distance. The scent hung heavy in the air. "We can't discount that fire either. I don't know where it's moving or how long we'll be safe here."

"Crap," she whispered, wrapping her arms around Maya and holding her close.

"How's your head?" he asked, gesturing to the goose egg on her right temple.

"Hurts like a son of a bitch," she said with a wry smile. "Don't suppose we have any ibuprofen in those bags that hasn't been ruined by all the water?"

"Probably not."

"Oh no." Isa stared at her hands, her expression stricken.

"What's wrong?" He crouched beside her. Her fingers were slightly pruned from their time in the water, but he didn't see any obvious signs of injury.

"My ring," she whispered.

She wasn't wearing any rings, but he had a hunch that was the problem. "Did it come off in the lake?"

"It must have." Tears glistened in her eyes.

"Wedding ring?" He rocked back on his heels, feeling a twinge of disappointment at the thought of her being married.

She shook her head. "It was my

15

grandmother's—a gold butterfly. She gave it to me before she…before she died. She said that as long as I was wearing it, I'd always be able to feel her with me." She blinked rapidly, her face tinged pink.

Aw, hell. "I'm sorry, Isa."

"Yeah, me too." She looked down at her hands and blew out a breath. "But I'd rather my ring be at the bottom of the lake than either of us. So what next?"

Nate felt an irrational urge to dive back into the lake and look for her lost ring. "We should probably take stock of our supplies."

"I agree."

He set their waterlogged bags on the ground between them. "What did you pack in yours? Rocks?"

"Dog food," she said sheepishly, pulling the backpack closer. "I packed a few meals for Maya in case we got held up overnight in Reno."

"Foods's good, but I think our first priority should be dry clothes." Because they were already freezing from having gone in the lake, and the temperature was only going to plummet as the sun went down.

"No dry clothes here," Isa said as she pulled a soggy pair of jeans and a yellow shirt from her bag.

"Let's take everything we have and lay it out in the sun. Hopefully it'll dry before nightfall." He took his spare clothes out of his bag, untied her sneakers and his loafers, and walked over to an outcropping of rocks. He spread it all out, then shucked his T-shirt and jeans and laid those on the rocks too.

"Um…" Isa said from behind him.

"I figure I'll warm up faster if I'm not in cold, soggy jeans. Plus, the more dry clothes, the better, right?" He turned to find her shamelessly checking him out in his boxer briefs, two spots of color on her cheeks.

"Right." She turned her back and started laying out her own clothes.

He headed toward their bags to begin going through the rest of his stuff. When he looked up, Isa was walking toward him, wearing nothing but hot pink panties and a flesh-colored bra, all smooth skin and soft curves, and he damn near swallowed his tongue.

***

Isa wasn't normally a self-conscious girl, but walking around in her underwear in front of a man she barely knew? Let alone a sexy, rich, CEO pilot who'd just crash-landed them in the middle of the mountains in a forest fire? Yeah, her day had gone from adventurous to WTF in the span of an hour.

Her head throbbed, and she focused on that rather than thinking about the eyeful Nate was getting as she knelt beside her bag. Nate, who looked outrageously delicious in his black boxer briefs. He was awfully tanned and toned for a man who worked eighty hours a week, but she was sure as hell enjoying the view. Maya—bless her—lay beside the bag exactly where Isa had left her.

Thirty minutes later, they had organized their stuff into piles. Between them, they had a dozen granola bars, a bag of potato chips, and two bottles of water, plus the gallon-sized Ziploc bag of dog food she'd brought for Maya. Nate had one of those gadgety pocket knives that was bound to come in handy, and a first aid kit that included several sealed—and therefore not soggy—packets of ibuprofen.

"Thank goodness." She snagged one and ripped it open.

"Not so fast." Nate reached for the pills. "If there's any bleeding in your brain, the ibuprofen could make it worse."

She gave him a look. "I survived a plane crash and swam out of an ice-cold lake. I'm willing to take my chances with a couple of ibuprofen."

Nate pressed his lips together but said nothing as she opened one of the bottles of water and swallowed the pills with the smallest sip she could manage.

"So," she said.

He gave her a long look, his expression hidden behind his mirrored lenses. "So."

"I've watched enough *Survivorman* to know we should probably be building a shelter by now," she said.

"*Survivorman*? Is that the show where the guy pretends to be lost in the wilderness?"

"Les Stroud, yes, and he teaches you how to survive until you're rescued."

Nate looked skeptical. "I don't know how accurate a TV show like that is."

"Well, let's hope we're not out here long enough to find out. And on that note, I personally am in favor of making some kind of big SOS sign out here in case a rescue plane flies by."

"Agreed. And since we don't have any way to start a fire, we should probably look for running water too. It would be safer to drink than the water from the lake."

"Okay." She climbed to her feet. "What first?"

"Why don't you work on the SOS while I scout locations for a shelter?"

Since it didn't seem like Maya was going to make a run for it, Isa unclipped the leash from her collar so that the poor dog didn't have to drag it around. She followed at Isa's heels as she gathered sticks and whatever else she could find to make her sign.

The lake before her was so pretty, it belonged on a postcard. Its glittering surface reflected the blue sky above and snowcapped mountains visible in the distance. She wanted to sit and take it all in, but as she started arranging sticks into the shape of an enormous S, something in her brain seemed to click into place. Like *oh shit*, this is really happening.

Nate's plane—and her butterfly ring—were at the bottom of that lake. They were stranded in the middle of nowhere with a forest fire nearby, and search and rescue might not even know where to look for them. She was going to spend the night somewhere out here, maybe more than one night, maybe…

Nope, she wasn't going there yet. She forced herself to focus on the present. She'd build the most amazing SOS ever, and a rescue plane might even find them before nightfall. After what felt like hours—and with the pain in her head blissfully reduced thanks to the ibuprofen—she walked around the finished product, surveying her work with a smile.

"What the hell is that?" Nate said from behind her.

Startled, she tripped and fell flat on her ass in the middle of the O.

CHAPTER THREE

NATE worked hard to contain his grin. Not because she'd fallen, but because she'd gathered fucking wildflowers to decorate her SOS signal. Bright purple and yellow flowers peeked out from between the pine boughs she'd carefully arranged. If that didn't perfectly illustrate Isa's personality, he didn't know what did.

She scrambled to her feet, planting her hands on her hips. "What?"

"You made it pretty," he said, allowing the grin to surface.

"No, I didn't." She narrowed her eyes at him. "I made it *colorful*, as in easier to see from the sky."

Okay, point taken. "Nice job."

Her hair had dried while she worked, and it

hung around her shoulders now in loose curls. Combined with the fact that she still wore nothing but her bra and panties, standing in the middle of her flower-filled SOS signal, she had just redefined the look of his fantasy woman.

"How did you make out with the shelter?" she asked.

But all he'd heard was "make out," and damn, it had really been too long since he'd gotten laid, because he was acting like a Neanderthal right now. "Want to take a look?"

She nodded, falling into step beside him as he led her away from the lake. About a hundred yards into the woods, they came to the fallen tree he'd used as the base for their shelter. He'd laid branches over it and woven pine boughs through, making a roof. The floor was heaped with heavy pine straw to protect them from the cold ground below.

"It's…small," Isa said from behind him.

"That's the idea, right? Should keep us warmer."

"Right." She crossed her arms over her chest.

"With any luck, search and rescue will find us tomorrow." In the meantime, though, it would definitely be awkward to crawl into this tiny shelter together tonight.

"So what now?" she asked.

"Sun's getting low. We should probably finish up whatever we want to do around here so we can tuck into the shelter once it gets dark. We don't have a fire, and I don't know about you, but I'm not wild about wandering around out here in the dark."

Her eyes widened. "There are bears out here,

22

right?

Bears. Coyotes. Mountain lions. "Nothing out here messes with people very often. We should be fine."

She shivered. "I'm going to go check on my clothes. It's already getting cold."

"Good idea."

They walked to the rocks where they'd left their clothes. His jeans were still damp, but his khaki shorts were dry, so he put those on with a T-shirt. Isa put on the black leggings and long-sleeved purple shirt she'd worn earlier.

"So much better," she said, rubbing her arms.

Nate's belly rumbled loudly. "Time to ration out some granola bars?"

"Definitely." She led the way to their bags. "Tomorrow, we could forage for food while we wait to get rescued."

"Not sure what we'll find." Nate handed her a granola bar and took one for himself.

"I told you I've watched a lot of *Survivorman.* We could look for dandelions, clover, all kinds of things. We could try fishing too, but I'm not sure if I could ever get hungry enough to eat a raw fish." She scrunched her nose.

"Let's hope we don't find out." Search and rescue would be out tomorrow looking for them, but would they know where to look? The forest fire complicated things. The scent of smoke hung heavy in the air.

Isa scooped a handful of dog food and set it on the ground for Maya, who began to gobble it down.

23

"I wonder if she knows how to hunt," Isa said thoughtfully, watching the dog.

"She might. If we don't get rescued soon, I guess we'll find out."

After they'd finished eating, they washed up by the lake, making use of the fact that they had toothbrushes and other basic hygiene items with them. They both put on their jackets, and then he packed everything into their bags and covered them with rocks to keep bears out. He and Isa separated briefly to answer nature's call before heading into the woods together to the shelter.

"Ladies first." He motioned toward it.

"First time I've ever spent the night with a man on the same day we met," she said with a nervous laugh. She scooted inside, rolling over so that she faced him. "It's not half-bad."

"Could be worse." He lowered himself in next to her and called to the dog.

Maya climbed in and curled up by their feet, and Nate positioned a pine bough over the entrance, sealing them in.

"How's your head?" he asked.

"Much better."

"You tired?"

"No." She sucked her bottom lip between her teeth and stared at him.

He wasn't either. Despite their eventful day and the darkness falling outside, it was probably only about seven thirty, maybe eight o'clock. "So tell me about yourself, Isabel Delgado. Are you from Anaheim?"

"Born and raised," she said.

"And what do you do when you're not flying rescue dogs up the West Coast?"

"I'm a marketing associate at Spring Hill Designs, but I just applied for a promotion to marketing manager, which would mean flying all over the country to visit client sites. That's why I decided to work on conquering my fear of flying today."

"I didn't exactly help with your fear of flying, did I?" Even before the crash, he'd been impatient and preoccupied, thinking about his meeting tomorrow morning with the CEO of a Fortune 500 company he'd been trying to land as a client for years.

She shook her head. "After today, I'm never getting on another plane again."

"Oh, come on now. Don't say that."

"You honestly mean to tell me you'll fly again?" She sounded incredulous.

"I'll buy a new plane as soon as I get home," he told her.

"That's crazy! We could have died today."

"But we didn't, and after seeing how well that parachute works, I feel safer than ever in the Cirrus."

"I never knew planes had parachutes," she said.

"Most don't. It's part of what drew me to the SR22. Sure paid off today, didn't it?"

"You must be rich," Isa blurted. "You can just buy another plane?"

He laughed quietly. "Well, this one was insured, but yeah, I could afford a new one. I'm a single man. I own my own business, and I don't live an extravagant lifestyle. Flying is my splurge."

"Tell me about your company."

"Sequoia Group has developed a marketing platform to manage social media content for large corporate clients."

"And you created it yourself?"

"Five years ago." The culmination of years of blood, sweat, and tears and worth every damn moment.

"You've been flying for fifteen years and owned your own business for five. Just how old *are* you?" she asked slyly.

"Thirty-three."

"Hmm."

He could barely see her now that night had fallen, but the air between them seem charged with a new kind of tension, one that made him acutely aware of the closeness of their bodies and the fact that it had been close to a year since the last time he'd had a woman in his bed. "Does that make me an old man?"

She laughed, a rich, throaty laugh that did nothing to ease the lust building inside him. "I'm twenty-seven so no, I don't think you're old."

"Good."

A silence fell between them, heavy enough that he wondered if he was the only one feeling the tug of attraction between them.

"So why was a CEO from the Silicon Valley flying from Anaheim to Reno today, or did you just fly out of your way to help Maya?" she asked finally.

"Business," he answered. "I had a meeting in LA this morning, one in Reno tomorrow."

"Hope it can be rescheduled."

"I hope so too." Because a million-dollar deal was on the line.

"I guess we should get some sleep, huh?"

"Sure." But he wasn't the least bit sleepy. Hungry, yes. Horny as hell.

The darkness around them now was complete. He could only see the faintest outline of Isa's shape next to him in the shelter. The pine bedding that had felt so soft when he'd first spread it out felt hard as stone now and itchy against his bare lower legs. Maya was taking up most of his foot room. It was damn cold in here too, but there was no way he was snuggling up to Isa—especially not while he was still sporting a highly inappropriate semi for her.

It promised to be a long, uncomfortable night.

***

Isa woke with a start, disoriented as she stared into the impenetrable darkness around her. Her body shook from the bitter cold, and a dull ache pulsed behind her right eye because...plane crash...stranded...in a makeshift shelter with a sexy stranger. *Right.*

Something rustled nearby, and she heard the unmistakable sound of an animal sniffing.

It was outside their shelter. Like, *right* outside!

Nate must have heard it too, because the next thing she knew, he'd rolled on top of her, pressing a finger to her lips. Fear flooded her veins, a combination of hot and cold that made her skin prickle and her heart race.

She envisioned a bear ripping their shelter

apart to enjoy his midnight snack. Or worse, a mountain lion. Her chest heaved, flattening her breasts against Nate's hard, muscular chest. If she wasn't about to be devoured by some terrifying nighttime creature, she might take the time to appreciate the way his body felt on hers, so big and warm and—

The creature outside scuffed against the wall of their shelter with its paw, and Isa's heart did its best to claw its way out of her chest. She held her breath to keep from screaming. Nate had gone rigid above her, silent and unmoving, but she could feel his heart pounding against hers.

The animal outside whined, pawing again at the branch behind her head, and two things clicked into place in Isa's brain at the same time—that was a dog's whine, and Maya's familiar form was no longer stretched across her feet.

"It's Maya," she whispered, jittery with relief.

Nate's body relaxed against hers, but he made no move to get off her. "You sure?"

"Pretty sure." She was also pretty sure that her leggings were paper thin, and that hard thing pressing against her hip was Nate's—

"Flashlight sure would be handy right now," he breathed against her neck.

"Mm-hmm." Her pulse pounded in her ears.

Nate reached over. She heard a rustling in the branches behind him, then Maya crept into the shelter. "Gave us quite a scare," he muttered to the dog.

Maya curled up at their feet with a sigh.

Somewhere in the process of letting her in,

Nate's body had shifted, and now there was no mistaking his erection pressed against Isa's belly. A warm ache grew between her thighs.

"Sorry." He lifted his hips.

"Don't be." She wrapped her arms around his waist and kissed him.

His lips were warm and soft, and they parted readily, inviting her inside. She clung to him, kissing him with an urgency that bordered on desperation. His tongue moved against hers in a delicious rhythm that melted away all her fear and uncertainty, replacing them with hot, liquid lust.

Nate lifted his head. "Isa, what are we doing?"

"Kissing?"

"You told me earlier you aren't the kind of girl to take a guy to bed on the first date." He rolled to the side, breaking the contact between them.

"I'm not." She struggled to catch her breath. Between thinking she was about to be eaten, and then sharing that blistering kiss with Nate...

"I won't deny I'm attracted to you," he said, his voice deep and gruff. Hearing him without being able to see him made the whole thing about a million times sexier. "But I don't think we should let adrenaline get the better of us and do anything we might regret in the morning."

CHAPTER FOUR

NATE woke cold, bleary-eyed, and grumpy. It had taken him six months to secure this meeting with his would-be new client in Reno, and now it might all go up in smoke because he had, well, gone *down* in smoke.

Sometime during the night, Isa had snuggled up against him—no doubt she was as cold as he was—and now her ass was pressed firmly against his morning wood.

Not. Helping.

He had it bad for beautiful Isa Delgado, which was a damn shame because since his divorce, he was only interested in sex for no-strings pleasure, while Isa was clearly looking for more. She was entirely too sweet for the likes of him.

Reluctantly, he shifted his hips away from her. A lot rested on today. He wanted to hear a search and rescue chopper whirling overhead, but the forest around them was silent. Too silent. Why weren't the birds chirping?

At his feet, Maya lifted her head and let out a low whine. Nate knew how she felt. He had a bad feeling as he slipped out of the shelter, as careful as he could not to disturb Isa. He walked to the rocky outcrop beside the lake, taking in the smoke-filled sky above. Either the wind had shifted, or the fire had drawn closer, or both.

It was a double dose of bad news because choppers wouldn't be able to spot them from above through all that smoke, and it was no longer safe to hang around waiting to be rescued. He bent to rub Maya, who had followed him out.

Isa walked toward them through the trees, looking beautifully rumpled from their night in the woods. He reached out and plucked a clump of pine needles from her hair.

"Good morning," she said with a shy glance.

Was she regretting their midnight kiss? "Morning."

"That's not good, right?" She gestured toward the sky. A thick wall of smoke obscured the far side of the lake and the mountain peaks beyond.

"Nope."

"What should we do?"

"Rescue protocol says we should stay put and wait for them to find us, but with that fire coming at us? I think we might need to get moving and try to rescue ourselves."

She stood there for a few seconds, sucking in deep breaths, fear swimming in her wide brown eyes. Then she swallowed hard and nodded. "I agree."

"Okay, then." He tossed her a granola bar and ripped open another one for himself. Four of their twelve bars were now gone, but he still thought it wise to put some food in their bellies to help them put as much distance between themselves and the fire as possible.

Too bad the granola bar did little to ease the hunger clawing inside him.

Isa fed another handful of dog food to Maya, and then they packed up. He slung his duffel bag over his shoulder, and she shrugged into her backpack.

"I saw a stream over that way when I was looking for stuff for the SOS sign yesterday," she said, pointing to the left. "It seems to be heading away from the fire, and sticking close to water is always a good idea, right?"

"I think it sounds like the way to go," he agreed.

With a nod, she led the way. They crossed the rocky shoreline of the lake to the stream she'd found. It was perfect for two reasons. First, water always flowed downhill, which meant that hopefully it would lead them out of the mountains. And also, water from the swiftly moving stream ought to be okay to drink. Boiling it would be better, but he'd rather risk drinking it than go thirsty.

"One thing you should know about me," Isa told him as they left the lake behind.

"What's that?"

"I'm stubborn to a fault. And I've decided

32

that we're getting out of this in one piece, which means I won't stop until I make it happen."

He grinned in spite of himself. "All right, then."

She scrambled over a boulder and hopped down to the stream bank. "How far do you think we are from civilization?"

"Honestly? I have no idea. The Sierras are full of hiking trails. If we're lucky, we could stumble on something today."

"We haven't been very lucky so far." She glanced over her shoulder at the curtain of smoke behind them.

"I disagree. We walked away from a plane crash in the middle of some seriously dangerous terrain."

"That wasn't luck," she said. "That was skill. *Your* skill."

"Partially."

They walked in silence for a while. The stream had leveled out, and they were able to walk along its pebbled edges with little difficulty. Maya trotted beside them, sometimes bounding off into the bushes after a critter that had caught her eye. Nate hoped the dog caught something. He and Isa might be able to forage for edible plants while they were out here, but Maya would be on her own once the dog food ran out.

"Oh, look!" Isa called out. "Cattails. Les Stroud says they're pretty tasty and nutritious."

"You're big on your *Survivorman*, aren't you?"

"Call me an armchair survivalist."

"Well, Miss Armchair Survivalist, you just

might save our butts out here, so nice going."

"Thanks." She tossed him another shy smile.

They reached the area where the stream widened into a marshy expanse, allowing the cattails to grow. Nate took off his shoes and socks and stepped into the cold muck barefoot. He pulled out his Swiss Army knife, but the first cattail he grabbed came right out of the mud with little resistance. So did the second.

"Grab a bunch," Isa said. "We can take them with us."

"Yes, ma'am." In a matter of minutes, he had an armful of cattails and waded back with them to shore. "So which part do we eat?" His empty stomach gurgled hopefully.

"The whole thing's edible," she told him, "but I think you're supposed to soak the roots to get the starch out or else they can give you a stomach ache, so maybe we should start with the stems."

She took a stalk from him, and he set the rest down on the grassy bank. She tugged at it, and the outer layer came off, revealing a shoot inside that looked somewhat like celery. Following her lead, he removed the outer layer from more of the shoots. When they'd finished, they had a sizeable pile. He used his knife to slice off the roots and set them aside.

Isa picked up the remaining shoots and walked over to the water to rinse them. Since this was her idea, he decided to let her keep on leading the way. She washed them all and laid them on a flat rock, then handed one to him and took another for herself.

"Here goes nothing." With a quick smile, she

34

bit off the end, chewed, and swallowed. "I might not be a fan if I wasn't so hungry, but you know, it's not half-bad."

"All right then." He took a hearty bite of his cattail. He'd expected it to be mostly flavorless, like celery, but it tasted more like a cucumber. A bitter cucumber. He was too hungry to care. He devoured three stalks, while Isa did the same.

Maya pounced in and out of the remaining cattails, looking very wolf-like with her thick, gray coat out here in the wilderness. She emerged with a small snake in her mouth. Isa let out a squeak, jumping backward.

He steadied her. "I'm glad she was able to catch herself some lunch."

"Will she eat it, you think?"

"We'll see." He watched as the dog played with the snake before finally settling down to business. She chewed and ate the whole thing. "Good girl," he said softly.

"We're off to a good start," Isa said as she helped him wrap up the rest of the cattails and put them in his duffel bag. She glanced up at the smoky sky. "If only we knew we were moving in the right direction."

***

"What if I climb that tree and have a look around?"

Isa looked at the tree Nate was pointing at. It was tall and straight, with plenty of branches. "Don't you dare fall and get hurt."

35

He gave her a mock-hurt look. "You underestimate me. I was a Boy Scout."

"Be careful." She watched as he gripped a branch and hauled himself into the tree. At first, she was just enjoying the view of his very fine ass as he climbed, but the higher he got, the more nervous she felt. If he fell...

She did *not* want to do this on her own.

Plus, she kind of liked his rich, plane-flying ass. A branch snapped, and her heart jumped into her throat. But Nate was still climbing, and he was ridiculously high.

"See anything?" she called.

"A lot of trees," he yelled back.

Trees. Well, she would rather he spot a luxury resort around the next bend, but trees were better than fire, in any case. Nate stopped near the top of the tree and spent several minutes craning his head in all directions before he started back down.

"Well?" she asked when he'd finally reached the ground.

"Good news and bad news. Good news is that I see a lot of smoke behind us but no flames. Bad news is that I don't see any signs of civilization anywhere, and there's a cliff up ahead of us."

"A cliff?" Her stomach tightened.

"We're going to have to leave the stream and skirt around it."

"All right."

"Better get moving. The sun's directly overhead, which means our daylight hours are half-over."

She turned and led the way. Truthfully, she

was exhausted and more than a little bit disheartened by Nate's news. Her head ached and so did her stomach. She might have overdone it on the cattails, but she'd been so hungry, she'd barely tasted them.

They came around a bend, and the cliff Nate had spotted came into view. It was a sheer drop, at least a hundred feet. The water roared as it plunged over the waterfall to the rocks waiting below.

"I feel like I need to send a little boat over it," she said. "Just to see what happens."

He gave her an incredulous look. "A boat?"

"A stick boat."

"You're something, Isa Delgado," he said with a smile, shaking his head.

"Something good, I hope." She grabbed a nearby stick and chucked it into the center of the stream. Then she crept close enough to the edge to watch it fall. The stick disappeared from sight as it went over, popping up about thirty seconds later in the middle of the pool below. "Sweet!"

Behind her, Nate chuckled. He took a long drink from his water bottle, then bent and filled it from the rushing water before them. Isa did the same. Then they turned around and left the stream behind.

And that was scary.

They plunged through heavy undergrowth, pushing their way into the forest beyond. Overhead, a hawk called, and she shivered. It sounded somehow ominous out here.

"What I wouldn't give for a big slice of pizza right now," she said to break the silence. Just thinking about it made her mouth water and her stomach grumble.

"Only a slice?" Nate gave her an amused look. "I could eat the whole pie."

"Mm, pie…with ice cream on top. Or, even better, a whole plate of my mom's homemade churros."

"I've heard of them, but I've never had one. What are they like?"

"Heaven," she answered with a smile. "They're crunchy on the outside but melt-in-your-mouth soft inside. Like a stick of fried dough, rolled in cinnamon sugar."

"Sounds delicious."

"If we make it out of here—" She pressed her lips together. She'd almost said she would make a batch for him, but she and Nate didn't know each other in real life. "When we get out of here, you should try them."

"I'll be sure to."

They walked on, picking up speed as the undergrowth thinned out around them.

"My mom's specialty is raspberry soufflé," he said after a few minutes. "It's so sweet, I can only eat a few bites, but damn is it delicious."

"I love soufflé." And all this talk of desserts was making her even hungrier. It had been a full twenty-four hours now since the crash, and they were no closer to being rescued. Maybe even farther now that they'd left the lake behind. She forced back the panic swelling inside her chest.

She couldn't stop thinking about her family back home in Anaheim. By now, they must know that her plane had crashed. She tried to imagine how she'd feel in their position, if one of her sisters had gone missing like this...the fear, the worry. If only she could let them know that she was all right. Why hadn't they stumbled across a hiking path or at least seen a rescue plane by now?

They reached a gentler version of the cliff they'd left behind. It was still pretty steep, though, and dotted with boulders of various sizes. Carefully, they began to pick their way down the incline. Isa kept her focus on her feet, shaking off her melancholy thoughts. She stepped onto a rounded rock, and the ground seemed to give out beneath her. She grabbed wildly for Nate's arm as she pitched forward, but her fingers grasped only air. Her face smacked into the pine-strewn earth, and then she was tumbling like the stick she'd tossed earlier toward the bottom.

CHAPTER FIVE

"ISA!" Nate skidded after her as she tumbled toward the bottom of the slope. His heart plunged right along with her. By the time he'd reached her, she was sitting up, eyes wide. He dropped down beside her. "Are you okay?"

"I—I think so." She was covered in leaves and pine straw, her face scratched and bleeding.

He brushed a hand against her cheek. "Scared the life out of me when you fell."

"That makes two of us." She trembled beneath his touch, her face pale.

"Sure you're okay?"

"I probably don't want to count how many scrapes and bruises I just got, but I don't think it's anything more serious than that."

"And you said you weren't lucky." He

extended a hand to help her up.

She took it and yelped with pain. "Might have landed wrong on my arm."

"Okay. Better let me check you over. The good news is that we have a first aid kit, so hopefully I can patch up anything that needs patching."

Isa scrambled to her feet, holding her right wrist against her chest. Maya sniffed at her, whining low in her throat.

"She's awfully protective of you," he commented. "You still going to take her to that rescue in Oregon?"

"My apartment in Anaheim doesn't allow dogs over thirty pounds." She winced as he took her right arm between his palms. "And anyway, Huskies aren't apartment dogs. She needs a big yard to run around in and some snow."

"True enough." He gingerly felt her wrist. It was red and slightly swollen, but nothing felt out of place as far as he could tell. "I don't think it's broken. Probably just sprained."

"Okay." Isa still looked shaky.

He wrapped his arms around her, pulling her in for a hug. "Awfully damn glad you're still in one piece."

"Me too."

They stood there for a long minute, just holding on to each other. This was no pleasure hike. If she'd been seriously injured, he couldn't have called for help. Finally, Isa slid out of his arms and turned, reaching for her backpack.

There was a large rip in the back of her leggings, revealing a flash of her pink panties and

41

another nasty-looking scrape. He averted his eyes. "You might want to change into your jeans."

She felt the rip and doubled over in laughter. "I don't know, maybe the rescuers will look harder for us if I flash them."

Nate grinned. Leave it to Isa to make him laugh at a time like this. He took the Ace bandage out of the first aid kit and carefully wrapped her arm.

"I think I earned myself another one of these," she said, snagging a packet of ibuprofen out of the kit.

"I'd say you have."

"And I'm going to go put on my jeans now," she said, her cheeks flushing pink.

"You do that." He turned his back to give her some privacy, trying desperately not to think about her ass in those pink panties. For a long minute, there was nothing but the sound of rustling clothes, during which he tried and failed to keep his mind out of the gutter.

"Um," Isa said from behind him. "I need a little help."

He turned, his gaze snapping automatically to her unfastened jeans.

"I can't get the button." She held up her bandaged wrist.

"On it." He buttoned her jeans, forcing himself to remain strictly professional, even when his fingertips brushed against the warm, tender skin of her stomach.

"Thanks," she said, sounding breathless.

"Any time. Ready to get moving?" Because as much as he'd like to stay here and let her rest, they needed to keep moving and get back to the stream.

She nodded, leading the way with Maya at her side. Occasionally, the dog would dart off into the woods for minutes at the time, but generally she'd stayed close to them throughout their journey, and thank goodness for that. Not only were the odds better for all three of them if they stuck together, but he figured Maya was handy to have around. Dogs were much more in tune with nature. If danger was out there, she'd likely know before he or Isa did.

Right now, he just wanted to make it through the day. They'd face tomorrow when it came. Soon, the sound of rushing water reached them through the trees.

"Thank goodness," Isa muttered, picking up her pace.

No kidding. They'd wasted lot of time detouring around that waterfall. The cattails had temporarily curtailed his hunger, but now his stomach ached for something more substantial. The sun—only a hazy blob visible through the smoke overhead—was dipping low in the sky by the time they reached the stream. They refilled their water bottles and kept walking.

"In another hour or so, we'll need to start working on a shelter for tonight," he said.

She nodded, her face set in grim determination.

Nate was tired, irritable, and hungry, but uninjured. Isa had a knot on her head from yesterday's crash and a sprained wrist plus who knew how many other bumps and bruises from her fall, and yet she hadn't complained once.

43

He respected that a hell of a lot. In fact, he respected pretty much everything about her.

If the situation were different...

But no. Discovering Kathy's infidelity had ended both his marriage and his belief in the institution. He was happier on his own. Not to mention, his business had tripled in income since the divorce, now that he was able to give Sequoia Group his full attention. There was no way he was giving up the single life now, no matter how infatuated he'd become with the gorgeous woman beside him.

The sun rested against the treetops ahead.

"I'm going to scope out locations for our shelter," he told Isa.

She nodded, crouching by the stream to fill her water bottle. He continued inland for a hundred feet or so, looking around. The trees were more sparse here, scattered amongst a bed of dried grass and pine needles. He found a rock about two feet tall and ten feet long with a flat side that might make a perfect wall for their shelter.

Isa joined him, hunting for fallen branches and pine boughs. By the time the sun sank below the tree line, they had a makeshift shelter in place. He heaped several armfuls of pine straw inside it, providing them as much insulation as possible against the cold earth beneath.

"You know, this survival thing is manageable during the daytime," Isa said from behind him.

"But the nights really suck," he finished for her.

"Yeah, they do."

"Supper?" He pulled out some of the cattails

44

they'd brought with them. The plants had turned dry and brownish now, but they'd have to do. He handed her several cattail stalks and a granola bar and helped himself to the same.

Six bars down. Six remaining.

Would they be rescued before their food ran out? Should they ration more strictly? Hell if he knew, but they needed energy to keep hiking twelve hours a day, so their meager rations seemed fair as far as he could tell.

"Only about a day's worth of food left for all of us," Isa said as she placed a handful of dog food on the ground for Maya, echoing his thoughts.

"We'll look for more tomorrow."

"Speaking of which…" She took his duffel bag from him and removed the cattail roots they'd brought along. "I'll soak these tonight to remove some of the starch, and we should be able to eat them tomorrow."

"Glad I had you along, or I might have starved." He said it jokingly, but it was true. The granola bars were hers. She'd been the one to suggest the cattails. All he'd contributed to their survival so far was a measly bag of potato chips, which wouldn't do much for them once they ran out of more substantial food.

Isa headed toward the stream with an armful of cattail roots while he put the final touches on their shelter. When he'd finished, he relieved himself behind a nearby tree and headed for the stream with his toothbrush.

"Do you think they're looking for us?" Isa asked quietly. She'd submerged their cattail roots in a

45

natural pool at the edge of the water.

"I don't know," he answered honestly. "The fire puts a crimp on things. I don't know how search and rescue operates under these conditions."

"Then we'll just have to walk out on our own." She stood and marched off in the direction of their shelter.

God, he hoped it would be that easy. The smoke had become steadily heavier throughout the day. How much closer would the fire draw overnight? He didn't know, but continuing to hike after dark was a disaster waiting to happen. Plus, they needed rest if they had any hope of making it out of here.

He brushed his teeth, splashed some water on his face, and made his way back to their makeshift camp. There were no loose rocks here big enough to bury their packs, so he'd just have to hope their meager stash of granola bars and cattails wouldn't attract bears. All the same, he left them outside the shelter. He'd rather any potential hungry predators make off with their granola bars than raid their shelter.

Isa was already inside. He put on his fleece jacket and climbed in after her.

"Going to be another cold night," he said as he handed her windbreaker to her.

"This rock is cold as shit," she said, gesturing to the rock behind her.

"So lean against me instead."

"I think we know each other well enough now to snuggle tonight," she said very matter-of-factly, even as his gut tightened at the thought. "It's only practical to conserve body heat. I was too cold to sleep a wink last night."

"Same." He wrapped an arm around her and drew her up against him.

Maya crawled into the shelter and curled at their feet. Nate placed the last bough over their entrance, sealing them in.

"How are you feeling after your tumble?" he asked.

"Sore," she answered quietly. "Nate?"

"Yeah?"

"I'm glad we're in this together. I mean—"

"I know what you mean." His arm tightened around her. "And I'm glad too. You're a hell of a survival partner, and a hell of a lady, Isabel Delgado."

"Same to you, Nathaniel Peters."

"I really want to kiss you right now." The words were out before he could stop them.

"I wouldn't stop you," she whispered.

"You should." He brushed his lips against hers, and his whole body lit with lust and need.

"Why?"

"Because I'm not looking to settle down, and you are, for one thing."

"I can kiss you without wanting to marry you, Nate." She pressed her lips to his. "And right now, it feels really good to remember we're alive."

"We're definitely alive." He anchored her against him, kissing her slow and deep as the hunger within him ignited to an inferno. His dick strained the front of his jeans, rock hard with his need for her.

They kissed until the air inside their shelter began to sizzle, until his pulse pounded in his ears and every cell in his body seemed electrified. Isa pressed

47

against him, so warm and soft. Her hips rocked against his as a soft whimper tore from her throat.

"Nate," she whispered, rolling on top of him. "What if we die tomorrow, and—"

"We're not going to die tomorrow." He gripped her hips, settling her so that his cock pressed between her legs. "And there is *no way* I'm having sex with you because you're afraid this might be your last night on earth."

"But I've been such a prude," she whispered. "Waiting to find 'the one.' What if it's too late?"

Holy shit. He froze. "Are you saying…"

"Oh God, no." She let out a hoarse laugh. "I'm not a virgin, not even close. But I've been cautious. Maybe *too* cautious. It's been over a year, and—"

"And that's no reason to have sex with me here tonight. You're right to be choosy."

"Please…" She rolled her hips, and he damn near came in his jeans.

"No condom." That was a lie. He was pretty sure there were a couple in his duffel bag, but it was outside the shelter, and no matter how bad he wanted—*needed*—her right now, he was man enough to put his own needs aside to do the right thing.

"Oh." She deflated against him. "I guess on the off chance we *don't* die tomorrow, that would be pretty stupid."

"We're not going to die." But far be it for him to leave her all hot and bothered. He moved his hand between them and unbuttoned her jeans.

Isa gasped into his mouth.

"How about a compromise?" He slid his hand

48

inside her jeans, cupping her through her panties, and holy fuck, she was wet for him.

"Yes," she moaned, thrusting against his hand.

He slid inside her panties, stroking her. She was so hot, so wet...

"Nate," she whimpered, grinding herself against him.

He pushed two fingers inside her, stroking in and out as his thumb pressed against her clit. She panted, kissing him with a kind of passionate desperation as he drove her closer and closer to the edge. With a moan, she convulsed around his fingers.

His dick pulsed so hard that, for a moment, he thought he'd come in his pants. But the vicious ache in his balls proved he was still locked and painfully loaded. It had been totally worth it, though, to get her off.

She collapsed against his chest, limp and panting. "That was amazing."

"Sure was."

"My turn?" She reached between them and gripped him through his jeans.

His hips thrust against her hand of their own accord. "As tempting as that is, we don't have any tissues. It's going to be cold as hell tonight, and it would be just plain dumb for me to spend the night in wet jeans."

"I can't leave you like this," she murmured, still stroking him.

"Yes, you can. I didn't expect anything in return."

"I have an idea." She scooted down, but the

shelter was too small to allow her to do what she had in mind, much as it killed him. Every time her face got near his dick, her back bumped into the top of the shelter.

He tugged her up next to him. "We're not going to destroy the shelter so you can give me a blow job. I'll survive. Honest."

"I know you will. You're a true gentleman, Nate. I really wanted to do this for you." She sounded so disappointed that it only made him feel worse.

"We should sleep. We have another long day tomorrow."

With a sigh, she rolled over, her ass pressed against his groin, and yeah, he *really* hadn't thought this through. They lay in silence for what felt like hours as the darkness around them grew complete. Isa shifted restlessly against him. He was still hard enough to crack stones and beginning to think he'd spend the whole night that way.

"I can't sleep with that thing poking me in the back," she said finally, laughter in her voice. "We're going to have to find a way to fix this for you."

"Tell me about your mother," he said wryly. "Or your least favorite teacher."

"I have a better idea," she whispered. "Give me your pocket knife."

He recoiled involuntarily. "Uh, I'm not sure I like your idea."

She giggled. "Have a little faith, will you?"

He couldn't think of a single good use for a pocket knife to cure his raging hard-on, but he must have totally lost his mind, because he pulled his Swiss Army knife out of his back pocket and handed it to her.

She wriggled around next to him, and he heard the sound of fabric ripping—or maybe being cut.

"What was that?" he asked.

"You'll see." She unbuttoned his jeans and pushed down the zipper. "Tell me when you're close."

"Baby, I'm already close." His cock throbbed in anticipation of her touch.

"Let me know when you're *really* close." And she wrapped her fingers around him.

He thrust against her, no longer caring if he spent the night in wet jeans, because Isa's soft fingers were worth every moment of future discomfort. She stroked up and down his shaft, adding a little twist at the tip that made him see stars.

"I've never done this with my left hand before," she murmured, and he felt a brief stab of guilt for letting her get him off while she was injured, but he was too far gone to argue now.

Her grip tightened with each stroke, harder and faster, and he pumped his hips to the rhythm she'd set, finally allowing himself to surrender to the orgasm building inside him. He was strung tighter than a bow and about to blow.

"Really close," he ground out, struggling for some last-minute reserve to keep himself from coming all over their only clean, dry clothes.

Her hand disappeared, and he bit back a groan at the cold emptiness left behind. Then she was wrapping something warm and soft around the head of his dick.

"What is that?" he asked, holding himself rigid and still.

"My panties," she whispered.

"Fuck. *Me.*" The mental image of her hot pink panties wrapped around his cock was too much. His hips jerked.

"A worthwhile sacrifice." She wrapped the fabric firmly around him and began to stroke again, faster, faster…

A guttural sound tore from his throat as he came, spilling his desire for her into her panties. Just picturing it made him come even harder.

"You're a fucking natural as a leftie," he gasped when he'd regained the ability to speak.

"Good to know." She wiped him off and tucked the panties somewhere near the bottom of the shelter. Maya let out a disgruntled snort at the intrusion.

He re-buttoned his jeans and pulled Isa against him, exhausted. With her in his arms, he fell into a deep, dreamless sleep.

Sometime later, he woke to the sound of an animal scuffling around outside their shelter. A long, low growl rumbled from somewhere below his feet. Beside him, Isa whimpered.

The beast outside snuffed at the pine bough directly over his head.

And this time, it was definitely not Maya.

CHAPTER SIX

TERROR slid down Isa's spine like a rush of cold water. At her feet, Maya let out another low, rumbling growl. The animal outside stopped moving, and the silence that followed was deafening. Isa could hear her pulse whooshing through her ears.

One second. Two. Three.

Maya burst forward, plunging out of the shelter. Something landed on Isa's face, and she swatted at it frantically until she realized it was a pine bough. For a moment, she'd thought the creature outside had pounced on her...

Then something *was* on top of her, but it wasn't a bear or a mountain lion. Nate's familiar weight settled over her, and she heard the soft click of the blade opening on his pocket knife. Outside the shelter, Maya growled again. The pine straw nearby rustled, and there was a loud snort right behind their heads that definitely didn't come from a dog.

Isa's lungs seemed to have collapsed on themselves. She couldn't draw breath, couldn't move. All that separated her and Nate from the animal outside was a thin layer of pine needles. She could almost feel the creature's breath on her neck. And Maya...

There was a thump outside—like a body hitting the dirt—and the sound of paws running. Whatever it was, it sounded huge.

Then silence.

She and Nate lay there for several long minutes, barely breathing, while her heart beat frantically against her ribs. Her skin prickled like she'd been plugged into a live wire. Where was Maya? Had she chased the other animal away? Was she hurt?

"I'm so scared," she whispered, her voice barely more than a breath.

Nate's arms tightened around her.

Outside their shelter, the night was still and silent. The darkness seemed to press in on her like someone had wrapped a heavy blanket around her face.

"I think whatever it was is gone," Nate said finally.

"Maya..."

"I don't know," he said softly.

"Should we—"

"We're going to stay right where we are, Isa. We can't do a bit of good for Maya if we're stumbling around out there in the dark with nothing but a pocket knife."

She knew he was right, but it was killing her to think of Maya out there somewhere.

"We should stay quiet, just in case," Nate said.

"Okay," she whispered.

He positioned her against him, facing the rock, leaving his own back exposed.

Protecting her.

She lay awake for the rest of the night, intensely aware of just how vulnerable they were to the big, bad world outside. The dangers of the forest had seemed somehow surreal just hours ago as she and Nate had fooled around here in the shelter, lamenting not having a condom.

How naïve they'd been.

Now she lay in his arms, shivering from the cold and the clammy fingers of fear that still gripped her, half expecting at any moment to be attacked by some unseen creature. Mountain lions probably didn't make a sound before they pounced.

She trembled until even her bones ached.

Somewhere before dawn she must have dozed off, because the next thing she knew, muted sunlight was filtering in through the gaping hole in the side of their shelter where Maya had exited during the night. Nate crawled out, knife in hand.

"All clear," he called.

She slipped out after him. At first glance, nothing appeared amiss. No blood. No fur. No sign of a struggle.

"I think it was after our food," he said, lifting his duffel bag, which had plainly been pawed at.

"What do you think…?"

"Black bear," he answered, pointing to a large paw print nearby.

Isa nodded, feeling as if the bear had just stomped on her stomach. A bear had been inches from her head last night…and Maya…

"We didn't hear any signs of a struggle," Nate said, obviously following her line of thought. "On the contrary, it sounded to me like Maya ran the bear off."

"Then why didn't she come back?"

"Can't answer that." Nate met her gaze, his brown eyes steady and sincere. "You told me she liked to run off a lot before. Could be she just decided to keep on running."

"Or she's hurt." Or worse…

Nate walked over and took her hands in his. "We have every reason to believe she can take care of herself, okay?"

She nodded.

"I had left our bags out here so that bears wouldn't come into our shelter if they wanted our granola bars. I'll put them farther away tonight."

"I'm ready to go home," she whispered, burying her face against Nate's muscular chest. She couldn't face the thought of another day lost in the woods or another night in a makeshift shelter.

"I know, sweetheart." He wrapped her in his warm embrace and held her tight. "Maybe we'll be in our own beds tonight."

Maybe, but he didn't sound very optimistic, and neither was she.

"And if we want that to happen, we'd better get a move on." He lifted her head and gave her a quick kiss.

"Okay." Reluctantly, she slid out of his arms.

They gathered their belongings and made their way back to the stream. Isa was looking for any sign of Maya, but she didn't see a single hair from the dog's fluffy coat.

"Maya?" she called. "Maya! Come here, girl."

Nate joined her, calling for Maya as they walked. Isa strained her ears for any sound in response, but the forest around them remained silent. Once they reached the stream, she and Nate both turned to look at the sky.

The smoke was closer. Darker. Its scent hung heavy in the air.

"Shit," Nate said.

The mood was subdued as they ate their breakfast of granola bars and sliced cattail root. They needed to cover as much ground today as possible. Never mind that she was already exhausted, mentally and physically. Her whole body ached from yesterday's tumble. And two days of nothing but granola bars and cattails was taking its toll.

Nate seemed to be feeling the same. Neither of them spoke much while they ate. She went around a bend in the creek for some privacy before stripping down in the chilly morning air. She washed herself off in the cold water and changed into her spare shirt, jeans, and her only remaining pair of panties. She could only hope they weren't out here long enough for her to regret sacrificing the pink pair in her shenanigans with Nate last night.

Despite her somber mood, she smiled at the memory.

Once she was dressed, she packed up her things and went after Nate. He'd changed too, now wearing a green long-sleeved shirt with his jeans. His face was coated in two days of scruff, which only served to make him look even sexier.

"Want me to rewrap that for you?" He took the bandage she held in her good hand.

"Please."

"It doesn't look too bad today. How does it feel?" he asked as he began to wrap her wrist.

"It's sore, but I'll live."

"Damn right, you will." He leaned in to give her another quick kiss. "Now what do you say we get out of here?"

She nodded, falling into step beside him as they set out alongside the stream. Smoke hung in the air like a cloud, stinging her eyes and burning her lungs. "Do you think Maya's okay?"

"I do." He took her hand in his. "If the bear attacked her, we would have heard it. But I don't know if we'll see her again or what will happen to her out there in the woods without us."

Out of nowhere, tears rose in her eyes. "I don't want to lose her."

Nate squeezed her hand. "She seems pretty good at looking after herself, and there's always a chance she'll find her way back to us."

They walked on for a while in silence, broken periodically as she called for Maya. An unspoken urgency seemed to be driving them today. The smoke was so thick…she kept glancing over her shoulder, each time expecting to see flames chasing after them.

"I really miss my cell phone," she said when

they'd paused for a drink sometime later. All their electronics had been ruined in their swim out of the lake. It was seriously disorienting not to know what time it was. She'd boarded Nate's plane on Sunday, which meant today was Tuesday, but beyond that, she had no clue. It felt like they'd been walking for hours, but they'd risen early. It might only be nine o'clock for all she knew.

Nate glanced up at the gray sky above. "Hard to see the sun today to judge time."

They set out again, but neither of them was moving as fast now as they had been that morning. Isa ached from her scalp to her toes. Between the bruise she'd gotten in the crash, the bumps and scrapes she'd gotten yesterday when she fell, two nights sleeping on the cold, hard ground, and a general lack of nutrition, she felt like a hunchbacked old person as she shuffled along.

"So you work in marketing," Nate said, again taking her hand as they walked. "What do you do for fun?"

"I go out with my friends a lot. We go dancing every Thursday." What if she wasn't home by Thursday? What if she didn't make it home? "I volunteer at the animal shelter on Tuesdays and Saturdays. I usually stop by my parents' house for dinner on Saturday after I leave. My mom cooks a big meal, and we all just show up."

A wake of homesickness swept over her so suddenly that it seemed to suck all the air out of her lungs. She paused, pressing a hand to her chest, struggling for breath.

"You'll be home by Saturday," Nate said

59

quietly.

"But what if I'm not?" She gasped for air. The smoke was all around them. If not for the stream, she wouldn't have even known which way they were walking. "Nate, what will we do if the fire catches up to us?"

He drew her in against his chest and held her tight. "Let's not think about it unless we have to, okay?"

"There's no way I'm going to burn to death in that fire," she said, her fists clenching into his shirt.

"Damn straight." He tipped her face up so that she met his eyes. "We didn't survive a plane crash, a frigid swim in a lake, and a bear to die in a forest fire. Now let's keep walking until we find a way out of here."

***

Nate gripped Isa's hand in his as they walked along the edge of the stream, coughing from the smoke. She was scared. They both were. The truth was, he didn't know how long they could continue to outrun the fire, but he'd never been one to dwell on the worst-case scenario.

They'd cross that proverbial bridge when they got to it.

In the meantime, they needed to make it through today and cover as much ground as possible. He only hoped they weren't walking *toward* the blaze. At this point, it was hard to tell which direction the smoke was coming from, but until they knew otherwise, he figured their best bet was to keep walking downstream.

"Your turn." She looked up at him. The bruise on her forehead stood out in stark contrast to the pallor of her face. "What do you do for fun?"

"I fly," he answered without thinking.

"I already knew that," she said, a faint smile returning to her lips. "What else?"

Good question. "Haven't had time for much else lately."

"Hmm," Isa said, giving him a look. "What about your friends and family?"

"My parents are in Fresno. It's about a three-hour drive, an hour or so by plane."

"How often do you see them?" she asked as they left the edge of the water to pick their way around a large outcropping of rocks.

"Once a month or so." Sometimes less often. He'd been awfully caught up in work lately, maybe too much so. "My mom has MS. She's in a wheelchair and doesn't get out much."

"Oh, Nate." Isa touched his arm. "I'm sorry."

"She's doing well, all things considered. I try to fly down and visit when I can." He blew out a breath. "I should go more often."

"I'm sure you do your best. And friends?" she asked.

"There are a few guys I meet up with for drinks every now and then."

"So you work sixty to eighty hours a week, fly your plane for fun, and only occasionally see your friends and family. It sounds awfully lonely."

He hadn't felt lonely before. Hell, he'd been too busy to feel lonely. But imagining Isa out dancing with her friends or joining her family for dinner every weekend left a hollow feeling in his chest. When had he turned into such a workaholic? "Something tells me you're never lonely."

"Heck no," she said. "I have friends or family stopping by my apartment almost every night. And I have two cats—Frankie and Lulu."

"They okay without you?" he asked.

She nodded, but the light in her eyes dimmed. "Pretty much everyone in my family has keys to my apartment, so I'm sure they've been looking after them for me. They must be so worried."

It was easy to get caught up in their reality here in the wilderness and forget the people at home wondering where they were or if they were alive. "I'm sure they are."

"My older sister, Valentina, is getting married next spring."

"You'll be there," Nate told her.

Isa's chin lifted. "Yes, I will."

They lapsed back into silence. There had been a lot less conversation between them today, mostly because they were just so damn tired. Periodically, they called for Maya, although he was starting to doubt the dog was coming back. This was their second full day of hiking on very little food—or sleep—and already his energy levels were ebbing. He was beat but knew it couldn't be much past noon, and since they had nothing for lunch and with the fire on their heels, they just kept moving as quickly as their bodies would allow them.

Hunger had become a constant ache in his gut.

They sky above grew darker, heavier, more ominous. He gripped Isa's uninjured hand, urging her on. She lengthened her stride, keeping up with him without complaint. They both understood the consequences for resting now.

Something splashed onto his forearm, and he looked up in surprise. "Was that a raindrop?"

Her brows knitted. "What?"

Another fat drop landed on his arm. "It's raining."

"Really?" Isa held her hand out. "Yeah, it is."

"This could be good news."

"I don't think rain can put out a forest fire, Nate."

"I don't either, but it might slow it down and give us a little more time to get out of here."

"Yeah, I like the sound of that."

Somewhere over the course of the morning, gray storm clouds had formed overhead, and he hadn't been able to distinguish them from the smoke already smudging out the sun. The initial drops soon turned into a downpour, and he and Isa paused to put on their jackets. Hers was a thin purple windbreaker that she wore with the hood cinched tightly around her face. His was a fleece pullover—no hood—that was soon soaked through.

He swiped rain out of his eyes. "Surely this is dampening the fire."

"It has to be." She peered at him through wet lashes. "I can't smell the smoke anymore."

"Me either." They walked on, hampered now by wet, slippery rocks and leaves.

"Okay, this really sucks," Isa said after a

63

while.

By now, he was soaked to the bone, and the constant splatter of water against his face was slowly driving him mad. The rain had started out as a blessing, but right now it felt like another form of torture. "Sure does."

"Even if it lets up soon, we're going to be soaked for the rest of the day," Isa said, her teeth chattering.

"Could make shelter tonight more difficult too."

"God, I hadn't thought of that." She bit her lip. "Lying in wet pine straw doesn't sound fun at all."

"Maybe we'll get rescued before nightfall."

"Maybe." But she didn't sound any more optimistic about that than he felt.

"We should try to keep an eye out for food sources anyway," she said quietly.

"That's a definite. So, Miss Armchair Survivalist, what else should we be looking for?" he asked, trying to keep a conversation going to distract them from their discomforts.

"I've been thinking about that a lot, trying to remember what I've seen Les eat on the show. He finds a lot of edible plants, but he also emphasizes that if you're not sure what it is, it's best not to eat anything. Clover and dandelions are definitely good, but I haven't seen any of those. We might get lucky and find more cattails. I also remember that pine nuts are edible, and there are a ton of pine trees out here, but I don't know exactly where the pine nuts are."

"Are they inside pine cones?" he asked.

"I think so. We could gather some tonight

64

and see if we find any nuts in them."

"Okay, that sounds like a plan. What else?" Because they only had four granola bars left, and he was starting to worry that rescue was nowhere near.

She glanced at the water to their left. "Critters in the stream, or just critters in general. Bugs, grubs, fish if we're really lucky."

"Reconsidering that 'no raw fish' stance now, are we?" he asked with a smile.

"It's starting to sound more and more like sushi with each passing day."

CHAPTER SEVEN

Isa hugged her windbreaker more tightly around her. Was Maya out there somewhere in this rain? Today had felt so much lonelier without her.

"It's getting late. Maybe we ought to try to do some foraging before it gets any darker," Nate commented beside her.

She cringed internally. Despite what she'd told him earlier, she had no desire to eat slugs, grubs, or raw, slimy fish fresh from the stream. But finding food was what she was best at out here, so she was going to do her damnedest to find them something for supper. "Let's do it."

"I'm going to turn over a few rocks and see what pops up." He stepped into the stream, fully clothed. "Not like I can get any more wet, right?"

"Right," she said with a laugh. She was soaked to the bone. Her sneakers squished with each step she took, and her wet jeans were heavy, cold, and starting to chafe her legs. "Okay, you take the stream, and I'll poke around here on shore."

She bent and began looking under rocks near the stream. The rain had faded to a drizzle now, but the damage had already been done. There was no way for her or Nate to dry off now and nowhere to build a dry shelter for the night. Her fingers were stiff from the cold, and the rocks were slippery as hell. She turned over as many as she could, finding nothing of interest.

Changing tactics, she wandered inland, lifting fallen branches and bits of tree bark. She lifted a big wedge of bark, and a shiny, brown salamander looked up at her. "Oh!"

"Find something?" Nate called.

"A little salamander, but I don't think I could eat him." He was too cute, and also too slimy… Her stomach turned at the thought of putting him in her mouth.

"He'd be more appetizing if we could make a fire and roast him first," Nate said.

"Ugh." She replaced the piece of bark, officially pardoning the salamander. A pine cone nearby caught her attention. Pine nuts. Now there was something that actually sounded appetizing.

A half hour or so later, she'd managed to gather three squirmy grubs and a handful of pine nuts—which were pretty easy to harvest once she'd figured out how to do it, although it would be much easier if the pine cones weren't wet.

"I hate to say it, but I think we should save our granola bars tonight." Nate sat on a rock beside her, water dripping from his lashes and coursing over his handsome face.

She pressed a hand against her empty stomach. They had four granola bars left, which meant he didn't think they'd be rescued tomorrow. "Okay."

"This might sound gross, but maybe we should eat what's left of the dog food."

She flinched. "But what if Maya comes back?"

"She hunts better than we do. It's something I think we have to consider if we run out of food completely. For tonight, we can share the nuts and grubs and finish off the cattail roots in my bag. Don't think they'll keep much past tonight anyway."

"The grubs are all yours," she told him, dividing the pine nuts into two piles.

"You need the protein, Isa. Here." He opened his bag, took out one of the remaining pieces of cattail, and wrapped a small piece of the stalk around one of the grubs, then handed it to her.

She stared at it as nausea rose in her throat. There was no way she could chew on a live grub, but if she swallowed it whole, she just knew she'd feel it wriggling around inside her stomach. "I can't."

"Yes, you can. Make Les Stroud proud." He nudged his shoulder against hers with a smile.

"Oh God, fine." She grabbed it from him, popped it in her mouth, gave it one quick chomp, and swallowed it down before she'd had time to think about what she was doing. A faint flavor of something like dirt lingered in her mouth. She gagged.

68

Nate handed her water bottle to her, and she washed it down gratefully.

"So how was it?" he asked.

"It tasted like dirt." She poured pine nuts into her mouth, grateful to replace the dirty sensation of the cattail-wrapped grub with the somewhat bitter taste of the pine nuts.

Nate popped the other two grubs in his mouth at the same time, making a face at her as he chewed and swallowed. "Nasty."

"Truly," she said after she'd washed down the pine nuts.

Nate did the same, then unzipped his duffel bag and doled out the last of the cattail roots. She took one and bit into it. It had dried out after a day in Nate's backpack, and she gagged again trying to swallow it. But food was essential to their survival, and she couldn't afford to be choosy. Dutifully, she choked down her portion of the cattail roots. "So where are we going to spend the night?"

"Been thinking about that." Nate looked thoughtfully at the stream before them.

"A soggy shelter sounds miserable." She hugged her knees against her chest, struggling to keep her spirits from plummeting. Tonight was going to suck so bad.

"I think maybe we should keep walking a little more and see what we find."

"Okay," she agreed, even though exhausted didn't quite cover the way she felt at the moment. She was so tired, her bones ached with it, but the thought of lying down in cold, muddy pine straw sounded about as appealing as walking some more.

She brushed her teeth by the stream before packing up to move on.

"Just a little farther," Nate said, sliding his warm, strong hand into hers. "Maybe we can find someplace drier to camp for the night."

"Maybe."

They walked in silence as twilight deepened around them. She missed Maya, missed her family, missed her warm, dry bed…

"See that tree up there?" Nate said. "I don't know the name of it, but we've passed a few like it today, and they seem to offer decent shelter."

She looked where he was pointing and saw a massive tree ahead with thick branches. It was too dark to see it clearly, but she was too tired to care. "Sounds good to me."

Nate led the way to the tree, and they ducked beneath its branches, crouching against the trunk. It was definitely drier here. They put their bags beneath them to keep from sitting on the cold, wet ground. Who cared at this point if their spare clothes got a little more wet? Everything in their bags was already soaked anyway.

She leaned back against the tree trunk, and it was such a relief to be out of the rain and off her feet that for a few minutes, she felt almost comfortable. Every now and then, a big, cold drop of rainwater would splash down on her head, but the tree—some kind of evergreen—provided decent cover.

"Okay?" Nate asked, wrapping an arm around her shoulders.

She nodded, her eyes already drooping.

"Wait." He rose to a crouch and pulled the

remaining food out of his duffel bag. "Just in case." He walked out of sight, returning a few minutes later empty-handed.

"No bears tonight," she murmured. Her stomach hurt from her meager supper of forest oddities, and her body seemed to have finally given out. As night fell around them, she nodded off with her head on Nate's shoulder.

When she woke, the first thing she was aware of was the pain in her butt from sitting on all the toiletries in her backpack. She needed to pee. It was pitch black around them, so dark she couldn't see her hand in front of her face. And Nate's hand was on her breast.

***

Nate woke sometime before dawn as Isa shifted beside him. The night around them was cold and dark, silent except for the splashing of the rain. His hand had slipped from her shoulder while they slept, coming to rest on her breast, the tight bud of her nipple pressing into his palm.

Under other circumstances, waking to find himself palming Isa's nipple would have made him the happiest man alive. As it was, his ass was numb from sleeping sitting up. He was cold, wet, hungry, and sore as hell.

"You awake?" he asked softly, lifting his hand back to her shoulder.

"Yes," she whispered.

"Not exactly comfortable, is it?"

"No." She sounded as miserable as he felt.

71

"What I wouldn't give for a hot meal and a dry bed right about now." He snugged his arm around her, hoping their voices would scare away any wildlife nearby instead of attracting it.

"And a bathroom," she said.

"Yeah, that too."

They huddled together, alternately dozing and talking, until the sky began to brighten overhead. As soon as it was light enough to see their way around, they crawled out from under the tree, eager to stretch their legs. They spent a few minutes freshening up, and he doled out granola bars for breakfast. Only two left. Not good.

"That was pretty much the worst night ever," Isa said, rubbing her eyes.

"Yeah, it was." And he really wanted to get them out of here before tonight. He'd like to go up another tree to scout their surroundings, but right now, everything was too wet to climb.

"I can't spend the day in these wet jeans," she said. "I'm going to have to wear my ripped leggings, and don't you dare laugh."

"I would never," he told her. Couldn't blame her for changing either. Wet jeans were a fate worse than hell. Despite the chill in the air, he changed into his khaki shorts, which were just as wet but ought to dry faster at least.

He'd never laugh at Isa in her ripped leggings, but it was going to take all his concentration to keep himself from checking out the intriguing flash of yellow panties exposed by the rip. If he had to prioritize his needs right then, getting her naked was right up there with dry clothes and food.

"It's Wednesday," she said as they set out. "Three nights in the woods is three too many. I don't want to spend a fourth."

A slight drizzle lingered in the air, but they were already so wet, it almost didn't matter. They walked alongside the stream, swollen now from all the rainfall.

"At least the rain seems to have slowed the fire," he said. Compared to yesterday morning, when the air had been thick with smoke, today he couldn't detect any trace of it.

"Thank goodness for that," she agreed.

Thick undergrowth slowed them down this morning. They had to wind their way in and out of the brush, sometimes detouring away from the stream to get around it. Isa was quiet. Her face was pale, and her eyes had lost some of their sparkle.

He needed to get them out of here. As soon as the sun came out, he was going to climb trees until he saw some sign of civilization, dammit. Around lunchtime, they stopped to refill their water bottles and rest for a few minutes.

"It stopped raining," Isa said quietly.

"Yeah." He sat on a nearby rock. "Keep your eye out for another tree for me to climb. I don't know about you, but I'm ready to go home."

"So ready."

They got to their feet and kept walking as the sun broke through the clouds overhead, bringing with it a much-needed boost in morale. The prospect of warming up and drying off was awfully damn motivational. They rounded a bend in the stream, and...

"Whoa," Isa whispered.

Whoa indeed. The forest before them opened up into a wide, green valley. The stream splashed over a gentle waterfall, rushing out into the open space beyond. The mountains swept aside in either direction, revealing some truly awe-inspiring rock faces. After days of seeing nothing but dense forest, the abrupt change of scenery was both jarring and awesome.

"It's beautiful," she said.

"Sure is."

"It feels like we're the first people to discover this spot." She laced her fingers in his.

"We might be." He was doubtful that there were many spots left in the Sierra Nevadas that hadn't been explored, but what did he know? He was a businessman, not a park ranger.

"As romantic as it is to imagine being the first people to stand here, I really wish there was a big, gaudy hotel out there interrupting the view."

He laughed. "Yeah, me too."

"Maybe we'll find some new food sources here, though." Isa led the way, scrambling down the incline toward the valley below.

"Food would be awesome." Because he was running on empty right now. As they left the shelter of the trees behind, he felt the warmth of the sun on his skin for the first time since the crash, and it felt fucking fantastic.

"That feels so good." Isa tipped her face toward the sky, arms extended.

"Sure does." The creek was wide and shallow here, dotted with rocks, its edges gentle and easy to follow. Outside the creek bed, the valley was lush with tall grasses and wildflowers.

She looked up at him, her brown eyes bright. "Would it be okay to stop here for a bit and rest, you think?"

He turned to look in the direction they'd come. The sky was still gray behind them, but it looked more like rain clouds than smoke. Was it possible the wildfire had changed course or even been contained? "I think it makes sense. We're visible here. We could make another SOS signal while we rest up and dry out."

"Yes to all of that." Isa unzipped her windbreaker and slipped it off. Then her gaze caught on something behind him, and her eyes went wide as saucers. "Oh my God, Nate. Look! A house!"

CHAPTER EIGHT

ISA could hardly believe her eyes, but there was definitely a wooden structure concealed along the tree line at the far end of the valley. She was racing toward it before she'd even realized what she was doing.

Nate was right on her heels.

The closer they got, though, the more she realized "house" might have been an overstatement. The cabin wasn't much bigger than a shed, and it had the look of an abandoned building, but it was man-made, and maybe...

She reached the door before Nate, stopping short at the rusted silver padlock securing it. Gasping for breath after her sprint, she knocked anyway. "Hello? Is anyone home? We need help."

"I think it's an old hunting shack," Nate said.

"Is it hunting season?" Her heart refused to give up on the idea of rescue.

"Don't think so. It doesn't look like anyone's here in any case." He jiggled the padlock, testing its strength.

Tears sprang into her eyes. For a few moments there, she'd thought they were safe. Reality was like a hundred-pound weight dropped on her shoulders. "Dammit."

"This is still good news," Nate said. "There may be a path leading out of here that connects with one of the bigger hiking trails, and anyway, I think the situation justifies us breaking in."

She couldn't help the gasp that escaped her lips. "Breaking in?"

"It doesn't look like anyone's been here in a while. I'll leave my number, and if the owner comes around, he or she can call me, and I'll repay them for whatever we use. Deal?"

She nodded. Whatever was inside the hunting shack was more than they had now, and if there was food… "Please let there be food."

"We can hope." Nate walked a few steps away and picked up a rock the size of his fist. He slammed it against the spot where the padlock met the door, and the whole thing splintered. The door sagged open.

"Oh my God." She stared inside, heart in her throat.

"Let's see what we've got." Nate led the way inside.

The shack was indeed just that…a shack. It was one room inside. A twin-sized bed was set in the corner on a rusted metal bedframe. Across from it was some kind of wood stove, with a couple of cabinets above it. She hardly dared hope...

Nate tugged open the first cabinet. It contained a pot, a tea kettle, and a few odd utensils. "That's just a tease," he muttered.

The next cabinet was the mother lode, though. Several cans were stacked inside. "Food!"

"Hallelujah." Nate spun them around to read the labels. "Raviolis, SpaghettiOs, baked beans." His eyebrows raised. "Spam."

"Spam?" She giggled. "Right now, that actually sounds delicious."

"Agreed." He shot her a dazzling smile as he picked up the can of Spam.

Her stomach gurgled in anticipation. "I've never been more thankful for meat in a can."

He popped the top and snagged two forks from the first cabinet, then handed the can to her. "Ladies first."

She inhaled the meaty aroma, and her mouth literally watered. She plunged her fork into it and pulled out a big chunk. It was salty and squishy and... "I think it's the best thing I've ever tasted."

"That might be the hunger talking." Nate winked as he grabbed a big bite. "Nope," he said around a mouthful of Spam. "This is my new favorite food."

They sat in the middle of the abandoned shack and devoured the entire can of Spam. When they'd finished, she leaned back, gazing longingly at the bed in the corner. She was so tired, and it looked so soft. "Think the owner would mind...?"

"I think a nap is definitely in order, but first we should lay our stuff out in the sun to dry," Nate stood and set the empty Spam can and forks on a shelf near the stove.

"Right." That made total sense, except she was so tired, she wasn't sure how she was even going to get off the floor. She spotted a towel on a shelf near the bed. It was folded as if it were clean, and she wasn't going to give herself the option to consider otherwise, because she had to get out of these wet clothes...now. "Give me a minute head start, okay?"

She struggled to her feet, grabbed the towel and her backpack, and headed outside. She walked to the stream and stripped down, not even caring if Nate peeked from the window. God, it felt good to be out of those cold, wet clothes. Her fingers and toes were shriveled like prunes, her skin cold and clammy to the touch. Several large blisters had formed on the bottoms of her feet from sliding around in wet socks.

She splashed some fresh water on herself, then wrapped the towel firmly around her. She rinsed her bra and panties and spread all her clothes on a large rock nearby. Walking gingerly now that she was barefoot, she made her way back toward the cabin, passing Nate on his way out.

His gaze dropped to the towel, then snapped back to her face. She flushed, tripping over her own feet as she hurried up the steps. The bed was made with red plaid sheets and a couple of worn blankets thrown over it. Nothing had ever looked so inviting.

Still wearing the towel, she slid into it, rolling toward the wall to make room for Nate. He came back inside a few minutes later, buck naked, and dear

79

God, his body was perfection. All those muscles, and his dick...

"Ready for that nap?" He climbed in beside her.

"Mm-hmm." As much as she wanted to appreciate the naked man beside her, her eyes just wouldn't stay open.

Nate tucked her in against him. The bed was so soft, and warm, and dry. For the first time in days, she felt truly relaxed and comfortable, and she was asleep before she'd even realized what was happening. When she woke, the sun cast an orange glow through the window, and *whoa*, she felt like a whole new woman.

That was the best sleep she'd had in days. The cabin might not have spelled rescue, but it was still a much-needed respite from reality. Nate's arm was around her, his hand resting on her belly with only the thin towel separating him from her naked body. The towel had come undone while she slept, freeing her breasts. She didn't care. She trusted Nate.

And she *wanted* him.

A restless ache grew between her thighs as she remembered that he was naked. He stirred behind her, and she wasn't the only one getting aroused, if the wood poking into her back was any indication. Feeling reckless and *alive*, she spun in his arms. The towel fell away, and her naked body landed against his.

"Well, hello." Nate's voice was low and gruff, his cock impossibly hard against her belly.

"Hi," she said, feeling suddenly shy because *hello*, they were both naked, but while she'd certainly never found herself naked in bed with a man she'd known for only four days before, this was different. She and Nate had gone through so much together. The bond between them went much deeper than physical attraction. They'd survived a hell of a lot, and they weren't safe yet.

"You're beautiful, Isabel Delgado," he murmured, his hand sliding down to palm her ass.

She felt beautiful beneath his gaze, despite the fact that she was bruised, battered, wore no makeup, and hadn't shaved in days. "You're not half-bad yourself."

"Damn nice way to wake up." He leaned in and kissed her.

The kiss started out innocently enough, but the moment his tongue swept into her mouth, she was a goner. She closed her eyes, losing herself in the sensation of his tongue sliding against hers, his hands on her bare skin, and the desire building inside her. She clenched her thighs together as the restless ache inside her began to throb.

"I don't know if I could ever get enough of you," he murmured as he nibbled at a sensitive spot below her ear.

"I want you, Nate."

"You've got me, sweetheart." He slid his hand between her legs, groaning as he touched her. "You're so wet for me."

"Yes. Oh—" The sensation of his rough fingers against her sensitive flesh was almost too much. She gasped, pressing her hips against him.

"Feel how hard you make me." He thrust his iron shaft against her belly, and the ache between her

81

legs increased tenfold. He kept stroking, grinding his cock against her belly as his fingers worked their magic, and she was too far gone to do anything but writhe against him, her hips bucking as he drove her right over the edge.

"Nate," she moaned.

"Come for me, Isa." He held her close, his hips pressing against hers as waves of blissful release rolled through her.

"Oh...wow." She went limp in his arms, still tingling with aftershocks. "You do that really well."

He gave her a long look through eyes hooded with desire. "I was just getting warmed up."

"Is that so?" She gripped his cock in her good hand, pumping her fist up and down his shaft. In some ways, it was a relief that they couldn't think about sex. It let her lose herself in this moment without worrying about how far to let things go. And she was really going to enjoy getting him off like he'd just done for her.

Nate drew her in for another kiss. "I have a small confession to make."

"Oh?" She kept her hand on him, thrilled by the way his cock pulsed beneath her grip and hoping his confession wasn't going to ruin this moment.

"There are two condoms in my bag."

"Oh." Her fingers tightened around him. *Oh.*

"I just thought you should know, but the decision is yours. I won't lie and say I wouldn't fucking love to make love to you, but if this is as far as you want to take it, I'm totally fine with that too."

Indecision whirled inside her until her head spun. "I'm not...I'm not sure."

"Then we'll stop here. Whatever happens between us in this bed, you've got to be one hundred and ten percent sure about it."

"I'm not one hundred and ten percent sure about anything that's happened since I got on your airplane," she whispered, her heart in her throat. Because on one level, she wanted to make love to Nate more than she wanted her next breath. But she'd been with only two men in her whole life, and she'd been dating both of them for months before she let them take her to bed. She'd thought they were special, but in just four days, Nate had become incredibly special too.

"That makes two of us." His arms tightened around her. "But I'm sure you would have caught my eye no matter where or how we met, Isa."

"Really?"

"Hell, yes."

"There's one other thing I'm sure of," she whispered.

"Yeah?" He looked into her eyes, scorching her with his gaze.

"I want you to come in my hand."

His cock jerked beneath her fingers. "Fuck, yes."

***

Nate was certain he'd never felt anything as wonderful as Isa's hand working his cock. That little twist she gave at the top had him seeing stars each time. He slid a hand between her legs, feeling how aroused she was again from getting him off. He stroked her, matching the rhythm of her hand on his cock, letting their hips bump together on each thrust, and it was almost, *almost* as good as being inside her.

"Nate," she whispered. "That's so good."

"I know it is, sweetheart."

She tilted her hips so that the head of his cock rubbed against her clit with each thrust. Then she threw her head back, moaning with pleasure. Her wetness slicked his length.

"Even better," he gritted, struggling to keep himself in check, because if this was the only time he had with Isa, he wanted to make every moment last. They groped and stroked as the shack filled with the sounds of their pleasure—her gasps, his groans, and the rhythmic bump and grind of their bodies.

"Oh God, Nate...yes!" She convulsed around his fingers, and his cock pulsed in rhythm with her release, his need fueled by her pleasure. Her fist tightened around him.

One hard, fast stroke of her hand. Two. And he came in a hot spurt against her belly. He groaned as the orgasm slammed through him, clutching her against him. They lay like that for a long time, panting. He was grinning like a fool. So was she.

"That was amazing," she said finally.

"Sure was." He reached for the towel she'd worn to bed, now twisted beneath them, and wiped them off.

Isa stared up at him, all mussed and glowing with pleasure, so goddamn gorgeous she took his breath away. He leaned in and kissed her, slow and deep.

"I don't know what tomorrow will bring," he

murmured against her lips, "but I'm awfully damn glad for today."

"Me too."

Fatigue crashed over him, and the urge to sleep with Isa in his arms was almost overwhelming. But, like it or not, this was not a romantic getaway. "As much as I'd like to lie here in bed with you all afternoon, there are a few things we really need to get done."

"We're staying here, right?"

"I think it would be foolish not to," he said. "In fact, as long as that wildfire keeps its distance, I think we should stay here until search and rescue finds us."

"I love that plan. This is seriously the best news since we crashed." She leaned in to give him another kiss, grinning from ear to ear.

He kissed her back, then climbed out of bed before he got distracted from the tasks at hand. First off, he walked outside to check on their clothes. His khaki shorts had dried, so he pulled those on, leaving everything else to keep baking in the sun.

His next priority was to get a fire going in the wood stove. He and Isa were going to be warm and comfortable tonight, and they could even send up smoke signals if and when search and rescue caught up to them. He found a small amount of dry firewood underneath the shack. Hopefully there were matches inside. As he climbed the front steps, he passed Isa on her way out, again wearing the towel tucked between her breasts. His dick stirred at the memory of what they'd done in bed with that towel.

Inside, he found a box containing three

matches. Not much to work with, but he was determined to make a fire. Failure was not an option. He arranged a few larger pieces of wood inside the stove, then added as much dry kindling as he could find, even using the box from their granola bars as tinder.

He lit the first match, touching it to the kindling. A flame burst to life in the paper and wood shavings he'd gathered. *Yes.*

But less than a minute later, it had gone out. "Dammit."

Using his pocket knife, he cut a piece of fabric off the blanket on the bed and added it to the kindling pile. He lit the second match and held his breath. After a minute or so, the fabric caught fire, sending flames curling up and around the nearest log. He nursed the flames with more bits of bark and fabric until at last the log began to burn.

Nate felt like Superman. He'd started a fire! Tonight, they would be able to enjoy a warm, comfortable night's sleep and even a hot meal.

He walked outside to tell Isa.

She emerged from the woods behind the shack, wearing nothing but the towel and her sneakers, a pensive expression on her face. "I can't find a path."

"No?" He'd hoped that the hunter or hunters who used this place might have tramped down a path to get here.

She shook her head. "I followed a few spots that I thought might be a path, but there was nothing definitive, nothing I'd feel comfortable following. I also made an SOS sign over there near the stream."

"Did you put wildflowers in this one too?" he asked with a smile.

"Of course I did." She rolled her eyes at him. "I want them to be able to see it."

"You know, I was getting discouraged this morning, but now I feel more sure than ever that we're going to get of this mess."

She gave him a sweet smile. "Me too."

"Even if the fire catches back up to us and we have to move on, we'll have had a rest and some real food, and we'll bring as many supplies as we can with us when we leave."

"Definitely." She went up on her tiptoes and kissed him. "But there's one supply I don't want to bring with us."

"Oh yeah? What's that?" He wrapped his arms around her to kiss her back.

"The condoms," she said, "because I want to use them with you here tonight."

CHAPTER NINE

ISA looked up from the wood stove, and her breath caught in her throat. "You…you shaved."

He grinned at her. "Sure did."

"Hot date tonight?" she asked with a smile.

"As a matter of fact." He bent down to give her a kiss.

"You've been holding out on me," she murmured against his lips.

"How so?"

"You have a razor, and you haven't let me borrow it?" She ran her fingers over his freshly shaven cheeks.

"The thought of shaving hadn't crossed my mind until tonight, but you're welcome to it."

"Why, thank you."

"So which entrée would you like for our romantic dinner—raviolis or SpaghettiOs?" He rummaged through the cabinet behind her.

"Surprise me." She stood and picked up the razor he'd left on top of his duffel bag.

"Isa." His expression sobered. "I'm torn on how to ration food for tonight."

"We could share the can of SpaghettiOs," she said, although the Spam was long gone now, and her stomach rumbled hungrily.

"We could, or we could eat a decent meal, get our strength back up, and go looking for more food tomorrow."

She was already nodding. "Let's do that. And we'll still have the baked beans. It's more than we had a few hours ago."

"Okay." He took the pot out of the cabinet to start warming up their dinner.

She went outside to make use of his razor down by the stream. If only she had packed makeup...or a skirt. But no matter how romantic tonight might feel, this was still a survival situation, and it was no time to be a girly-girl.

Maybe if she and Nate made it out of here, they could go on a real date. She could dress up for him, and they could go out for a nice dinner and eat until they were stuffed.

She smiled at the thought.

So what if he lived four hundred miles away? He loved to fly. He could fly into town for their date.

She was grinning like a fool as she shaved her legs, beautifying herself for her "date." Two condoms. A happy shiver raced through her. She

89

wasn't even sure why she'd hesitated earlier. She and Nate had already been through more together than most couples ever endured. She cared about him, she trusted him, and most of all, she *wanted* him.

Even if they never saw each other again after they were rescued, she'd never regret a moment of their time together. The rapport and the chemistry between them had kept her going when she was running on empty, and tonight would be incredibly special, no matter what happened tomorrow.

After she'd finished shaving, she washed off in the stream. She even got out her travel-sized bottle of shampoo and washed her hair, which felt *amazing*. After toweling off, she dressed in her purple shirt and leggings, then gathered the rest of their clothes to bring them inside. The sun had already sunk behind the tree line, and although their jeans and sneakers were still damp, they'd dry better in front of the fire than out here in the cold, dark night.

Before she went inside, she stood there for a few minutes in the darkening field and called for Maya. Why hadn't she come back to them yet? *Please let her be safe.*

Finally, she stepped inside the cabin and pulled the door shut behind her. "Of all the things I'm looking forward to tonight, having walls separating me from the bears and mountain lions is pretty high on the list."

"We are going to sleep so good tonight." He gave her another one of those wickedly sexy smiles, and her insides went all warm and fluttery. He poured the contents of the pot into a battered metal bowl and handed it to her. "SpaghettiOs for the lady."

"I think SpaghettiOs are about to become my new favorite food." She sat cross-legged on the end of the bed and began to eat. "Oh God," she moaned as the first bite of steaming-hot pasta passed her lips.

"I'm hard just watching you eat," Nate said.

Her gaze dropped to his crotch, where indeed a bulge had grown in the front of his shorts. Warmth flowed through her veins, pooling between her thighs. She took another big bite of her dinner and moaned again. "I will never take real hot food for granted again."

"Funny how it takes a situation like this to make you realize what's really important in life." He was still watching her intently, his gaze riveted on her mouth.

"For real. I've joked with my friends before about 'first world problems,' but if we make it out of here, I'm never taking any of that stuff for granted again."

"When," he said softly. "*When* we make it out of here, Isa."

She nodded as tears pricked behind her eyes. "When."

"Search and rescue will find us, and if they don't, we'll walk out of here ourselves."

"Yes."

"I want to hear you say that word a lot tonight."

The ache between her legs intensified. "I think you will."

"Food might be the best foreplay tonight," he said as he poured his raviolis into a bowl and began to eat.

91

Any other time, she would have laughed, but after four days of granola bars, cattails, and grubs, real hot food was practically orgasmic. They sat side by side on the bed, not talking much while they ate.

"Man, that was good," she said when she'd finished. She barely resisted the urge to lick the bowl. "I do feel a little bit bad, though. I mean, what if the hunter comes out here thinking he has a few days' worth of food waiting for him, only to find we've raided his pantry?"

Nate gave her a funny look. "Well, I didn't want to mention it before we ate since we really needed the calories, but these cans expired a few months ago. I don't think anyone's been here in years, to be honest, and if the owner does come back, he'll surely bring fresh food with him."

"Oh." She pressed a hand to her stomach, but nope, she didn't regret eating expired SpaghettiOs. Totally worth it to be free of the aching hunger that had gnawed at her insides for the last few days.

Nate finished his raviolis and took both of their bowls over to the shelf above the wood stove. "We'll rinse them in the stream when the sun comes up so that we can leave them clean in case the owner does come back."

She stared at his duffel bag, picturing the two condoms inside. "So you do this a lot—pick up women while you're traveling for business?"

He turned to face her. "I wouldn't say I do it a lot, but I usually keep a couple of condoms in my bag in case I meet someone at a hotel bar or something like that."

The idea of picking up a random man at a

hotel bar and taking him up to her room was so foreign to her that she couldn't quite imagine it. "So no girlfriend waiting for you at home?"

He came to sit beside her on the bed. "I may be a lot of things, but a cheater is not one of them."

"What kind of things are you, then?" she asked softly, staring into his brown eyes.

"An entrepreneur, a pilot...a workaholic." He paused before that last one, and something flickered in his eyes.

"You know what they say about all work and no play." The air between them seemed to ignite. They weren't touching, and yet her whole body burned for him.

"It makes Nate a lonely, horny man." He reached out to trail a hand through her hair. "You still want to do this, Isa?"

She nodded, her throat gone dry. "The last four days have been absolutely crazy, but this feels right. No matter what happens tomorrow, I won't regret it."

He leaned in and brushed his lips against hers with a kiss so gentle, so tender, that it melted away all her fears about tomorrow. For tonight, she wasn't lost. Tonight, she'd found something amazing, something special here with Nate.

She leaned in, kissing him back, drinking in the sensation of his mouth on hers, the hot stroke of his tongue, and the way his fingers tangled in her hair, anchoring her face to his. They kissed until her heart beat a frantic rhythm against her ribs and her chest heaved for breath.

Night had fallen outside the cabin, and the

only light now was the warm flicker of the fire in the stove. It set the mood perfectly, not to mention kept the air around them cozy and warm.

"This *so* beats last night sitting against a tree trunk in the rain," she whispered against his lips.

"Fuck yes." His hand slid down to cup her breast. "I woke up touching you like this, and I was too cold and miserable to even appreciate it."

"That was probably the worst night of my life."

"Mine too." He stroked a thumb over her nipple, sending pleasure rippling through her. "And since you've reminded me, I'd better check on the fire before we get too distracted."

"Yes." Because if it went out...well, they'd still be okay, but tonight was going to be so much better with its light and warmth to protect them. She stretched out on the bed, watching as he opened the stove, using the poker to adjust the wood inside before adding another log.

Finally, he closed it and stood, the fire behind him casting dramatic shadows over his profile, exaggerating the contours of his face, the muscles on his bare chest, and *whoa*, the bulge in the front of his shorts. He slid into bed beside her, his body brushing up against hers.

"Who would have thought an old, abandoned shack would be so romantic?" She slid her hand over his back, reveling in the ripple of muscles beneath all that warm, firm skin.

"Seems like you and I are able to make just about anyplace romantic."

She smiled against his lips, remembering their

94

bumbled attempts at romance inside their makeshift shelters. "Imagine what would happen if we went on a real date?"

"I'd fly you to San Diego and take you to this amazing little Italian place—"

"Nope. I'm never flying again, remember?"

"You should," he said, his voice gruff. "Don't let one bad experience hold you back, Isa. You don't seem like a woman to let fear win."

"I'm not," she whispered. "But I've lived my life just fine on the ground until now."

"And now it's time to spread your wings." His hand slid around to cup her ass, hauling her up against him. "So I'd fly you to this amazing Italian restaurant in San Diego, right on the waterfront. If you like seafood, I recommend the Linguini di Mare."

"That sounds delicious."

"It's got shrimp, scallops, and mussels in a spicy tomato sauce."

"Yum."

"We'd finish our meal with a plate of tiramisu," he said. "Afterward, we'd go dancing. You like to dance, right?"

"I love dancing," she whispered, her eyes sliding shut as she visualized the picture he was painting.

"We get our groove on, a little bump and grind on the dancefloor." His hips had begun to move to an imaginary beat.

"Yes." *God, yes.*

"We have a few drinks. What's your favorite?" he asked, his hips still rocking against hers.

"Piña colada with a pineapple wedge on top."

95

"If we're going to drink piña coladas, then we'll have to go for a walk along the beach afterward, let the saltwater breeze blow through your hair." He trailed his fingers through her hair, and a warm sizzle rippled through her.

"Yes," she whispered. "I can almost hear the waves crashing against the shore."

"We make out in the moonlight." He brought his lips to hers for another heady kiss. "Like this."

Yes, yes, yes...

"And then I'd take you to our hotel room overlooking the ocean, where I'd have a nice bottle of wine waiting, maybe chocolate-dipped strawberries too, and we'd put on some music in the room so that we could dirty dance the way you'd never dare in a crowded club." He slid out of bed, tugging her up against him.

They swayed together, and she could almost hear the music, taste the wine and the strawberries...

"And once we were alone in our room, I could do this." He tugged her shirt over her head, groaning low in his throat as he cupped her breasts in his big, warm hands. "Finding out you weren't wearing a bra would be one of the highlights of our date for me."

"Then what?" she asked breathlessly, leaning forward so that her breasts pressed against his bare chest. The scrape of his chest hair over her sensitive nipples sent a bolt of lust straight to her core.

"That's where the dirty dancing part comes in," he said, and she could feel him smiling against her lips. He slid one big, muscled thigh between her legs, and she whimpered.

96

"Like this?" she rocked her hips, riding his thigh.

"Oh yeah, sweetheart." He lifted her so that his cock pressed between her legs, and he was so hard... "And we dance until we can't dance anymore."

They moved together, swaying to the music only they could hear, their hips grinding together as their hands touched and explored. It was beautiful, and romantic, and *hot*. Somewhere along the way, her pants hit the floor, as did his shorts. He was naked beneath his shorts, but he made no immediate move to take off her panties.

"I've been fantasizing about these," he murmured, teasing her through the thin fabric.

"Really?" She gasped as he slid two fingers inside her panties.

"Mm-hmm. I love them almost as much as the pink pair."

The pink pair she'd sacrificed in their second makeshift shelter so that he could come into them. Desire shot through her at the memory. "Almost as much?"

"After tonight, it may be a tie." He thrust his cock against her belly while he stroked her with his fingers, and just like that, she came apart in his arms.

"Nate," she moaned as the orgasm slammed through her, leaving her breathless.

"Fucking beautiful," he said, holding her close until she'd regained her senses. "I love the sound you make when you come."

She made a sound? She probably should have been embarrassed, but she was too blissed out to care.

And his hard shaft pressed against her belly already had desire stirring inside her again. Smiling, she stepped out of her panties as firelight danced over their naked bodies.

"I need you so bad right now," he said with a groan.

"Then have me." She dropped onto the bed, pulling him down on top of her.

CHAPTER TEN

"OUR hotel room would overlook the beach," Nate said, keeping the fantasy date alive as he kissed his way over every inch of Isa's body.

"Of course it would," she whispered, gasping as he drew her nipple into his mouth, teasing it with his tongue.

"We'd have a king-sized bed, not that we'd need it since we'll be on top of each other all night." He let his hips settle on hers, his cock nudging against her, and sweet Christ, she was so hot, so wet. "One of those feather-top mattresses, so soft you could lose yourself in it."

"Yes." She rolled her hips, sliding up and down his length.

Sweat beaded on his brow. "And then I'd

make love to you, Isa, if you were ready."

"I'm ready," she whispered. "I'm so ready."

"Me too, baby." He rocked his hips against her once, twice, then reached for the condom he'd placed beside the bed. He sheathed himself, positioning his cock against her entrance. With one long, slow thrust, he lost himself inside her. Her hot, tight body gripped him as he slid home. "God, you feel so good."

"Mmm…" She wrapped her legs around his hips, drawing him deeper still.

"Christ, Isa." He withdrew and thrust again, swamped with sensation. His body shook, his control ready to snap. He drew a deep breath, forcing back the need rearing inside him. He would *not* go off like a randy teenager thirty seconds after getting inside her.

"Nate," she moaned.

He stroked inside her, slow and steady, while his body burned in the most excruciatingly wonderful way. Dipping his head, he kissed her, letting his tongue tangle with hers as their bodies moved together. With each thrust, he lost a little more of himself to her. Beautiful, wonderful, amazing Isa.

"We'd leave the music on," he murmured against her lips. "Something really sexy."

"Merengue," she whispered, "or salsa. Spanish music is all about sex."

"I need to listen to more Spanish music." He brought his hand between them, stroking her where their bodies joined.

"I'll play some for you." Her thighs clamped around his. "Oh God, Nate…"

"Come for me, sweetheart." He kissed her,

swallowing her moan. "Take your time and make it good."

"I'm so close," she whispered.

So was he. The orgasm building inside him was so big, he thought it might blow the top off his head when he finally came. He stroked her with his fingers while he pounded into her with his cock, loving every fucking second.

She tensed. Her body spasmed around him, and she let out a breathless sound of pleasure. He kept moving, thrusting into her over and over as she came.

"Yes," she moaned.

And just like that, he broke. Release pulsed through him in a series of blindingly hot waves, scorching him with the power of his need for her. He let out a strangled sound as he poured himself into her, then collapsed next to her in bed, completely spent.

"That was amazing," Isa murmured, her arm wrapped tight around him.

"Damn right it was."

"Nate," she whispered, resting her face against his chest. "If we get out of this thing alive, promise me we'll go on that date."

Reality slammed back into him, hard. "I'd love that more than anything, but I'm not sure it's a good idea."

"Why not?" she asked, disappointment dripping from her tone.

He looked up at the ceiling. "This thing between us...well, it's crazy and intense, and frankly, I want you so much I can hardly think straight, but in real life, I'm afraid I'd let you down."

"How?"

"I'm married to my job, Isa. I work long hours, and I love what I do. I live it and breathe it, and it doesn't allow for much of a social life."

"That's a weak excuse." She narrowed her eyes at him.

"I'm just trying to be honest."

"And I appreciate that, but now you've warned me, and I still want that date."

"You're stubborn," he said with a grin, drawing her in closer. "And I love that about you. I like pretty much everything about you, Isa, and I couldn't stand it if I hurt you. I used to think I could be the man you want me to be, but since my divorce, I just...I don't believe in marriage and happily ever after anymore."

"You're divorced?"

"Yeah."

"What happened?" she asked softly.

"She cheated on me." And he couldn't believe he'd just blurted that out. No one outside his immediate family knew what had gone down between him and Kathy. How could he tell people that she'd been so dissatisfied with him she'd turned to another man? The betrayal still burned like a freshly formed scab in his chest.

"Oh, Nate. I'm sorry."

"So am I, but...what I'm trying to say is that I don't plan on getting married again."

***

Isa thought Nate was a man who'd had his heart broken and his trust shattered, but how could he let his ex-wife's betrayal convince him that he'd never fall in love again? That was absolutely ridiculous.

"I don't remember asking you to marry me," she said in a joking tone, trying to lighten to mood between them.

He smiled, his arm tightening around her. "You know what I'm trying to say."

Yeah, she did. She just didn't quite believe him. "Just because you've buried yourself in work since your divorce doesn't mean that will never change."

"Maybe not, but I love what I do. Ever since I was a little boy, I've dreamed about owning my own company. I'm living my dream."

"Even if it means picking up random women in hotel bars for the rest of your life?"

"Yes."

She didn't respond to that because the man who'd just taken her on the most romantic (virtual) date of her whole life didn't seem like a man who could be satisfied with a lifetime of meaningless one-night stands. Or could he? She remembered the impersonal businessman who'd greeted her when she boarded his plane four days ago. He'd wanted nothing more than to deliver her and Maya to their next stop in Reno and be done with them.

Maybe life-and-death situations made people act out of character.

And maybe she ought to quit thinking about the future and savor this night with Nate before the

103

ugly reality of their situation reared its head again in the morning. For tonight, they were warm and dry. Safe.

"Thank God for this cabin." She rested her head against his chest.

"Yeah." His heart beat strong and steady beneath her cheek.

"I don't know if I could have handled another night in the woods," she said softly.

"Sure you would have. You've handled everything life has thrown at us so far, Isa, and you haven't even complained."

"I was just about to start complaining," she said with a smile.

"Like hell." His cock was hard again, pressing against her thigh.

"And you, lugging around the extra weight of those condoms without even telling me." She wiggled closer, bringing their bodies into alignment.

"They were really weighing me down," he agreed, rocking his hips against hers.

"Nate," she whispered as desire blazed inside her. "I'm so glad for tonight."

"Me too, sweetheart." He kissed her slow and deep.

Their bodies moved together as they touched and teased, building the heat between them to a slow burn. There was an unspoken urgency in the air, the need to make this moment last because they had only one condom left. So they kissed and touched, groping and stroking until she was about two seconds away from coming on his fingers. "Now, Nate. Hurry."

"Won't hurry, not with you." He reached over

and grabbed the second condom packet from the shelf behind the bed. He ripped it open and rolled it over his hard length.

She climbed into his lap, and he settled his hands on her hips, lifting her so that the head of his cock nudged against her entrance. Her body clenched in anticipation.

"Finally," she gasped as she sank onto him.

"You can say that again." Nate laughed roughly, his hands sliding down to cup her ass.

She sat still for a moment, just savoring the feel of him inside her and the crazy-hot sensations rolling through her. "It's so perfect."

"Fuck yeah." He bent his head to kiss her again. "But you can start moving any time now. I'm dyin' here."

She lifted her hips at the same time something scratched at the door of their cabin. *Seriously?* She grumbled as desire and fear warred for dominance inside her. Could a bear get through that door if it wanted to? "What was that?" she whispered.

"Not sure," Nate answered, frozen beneath her.

A high-pitched whine came from the other side of the door.

Oh my God. She lurched out of bed as Nate swore from behind her. "It's Maya!"

"Don't open that door unless you're sure," he warned.

She slipped into Nate's T-shirt and walked to the window. Sure enough, Maya's gray face and front paws came into view. Tears sprang into Isa's eyes. "It's her! Oh, Maya."

She flung the door open, and the dog bounded inside. Isa latched the door behind her and crouched to gather Maya into her arms. "I've been so worried about you!"

Maya licked her face, her tail wagging so fast, it was nothing but a blur in the dim light of the fire.

"Hey, girl." Nate crouched beside her, having buttoned his shorts before joining them.

And *dammit*, Maya sure had showed up at the worst possible moment. But Isa was so glad to see her that she could forgive the wasted condom. She checked the dog for any obvious signs of injury, but apart from some burrs matted into her fur, Maya appeared none the worse for wear after two days on her own.

"You must be starving." Isa walked to her backpack, retrieving the bag of dog food. She placed a handful on the floor and looked around for something she could use as a water bowl, but she and Nate had dirtied all the available containers making their supper. Then again, Maya would probably *love* to drink out of a bowl with SpaghettiO residue in it. She poured a little bit from her water bottle and set it down.

"Can't believe she turned up," Nate said, watching Maya scarf down the dog food.

"Maybe staying put for a little while let her catch up to us."

"Could be," he said with a nod.

"I'm so glad." Isa restrained the urge to hug the dog while she ate. It had been slowly driving her crazy, wondering what had happened to Maya, if she was still alive, if she was lost or hurt. To have her back with them only served as a further morale boost.

She and Nate had arrived at this cabin wet, starving, exhausted, and demoralized. Now, they were refreshed and more determined than ever to make it home safely. They'd come too far to consider any other alternative. They sat together on the bare, wood floor while Maya ate and drank. Nate tended to the fire. The night outside was dark and quiet.

"Guess it's time for us to turn in," she said. They needed to take full advantage of this opportunity to get a good night's sleep, because who knew what tomorrow would bring. But she was still restless and unsatisfied. If only Maya could have waited just a few minutes longer to show up...

Nate nodded, walking over to check that the door was securely latched. Then he turned toward her. "Just one bit of unfinished business to take care of before we sleep."

"What's that?" she asked, her voice gone breathless at the look in his eye.

In answer, he dropped his shorts. "We've been awfully good at improvising without condoms so far. Why stop now?"

CHAPTER ELEVEN

"WE do improvise without condoms really well." Isa giggled, snuggled against Nate's chest as they lay tangled together in the aftermath of yet another mind-blowing orgasm.

"Now we sleep." He tightened his arm around her, sated and satisfied in a primal way, but also fiercely protective of the woman in his arms. He wished he could whisk her home to safety tomorrow, that they didn't have to wait around and hope that search and rescue found them.

"Mm-hmm." Her eyes were already drifting shut.

He pulled the blankets over them and motioned to Maya to join them in bed. The dog curled over their feet. The cabin was comfortably warm thanks to the wood stove, with a flickering glow from the fire. Right then, this abandoned little shack felt like the Four Seasons.

With Isa in his arms and Maya at his feet, he slept deep and dreamless. When he woke, the sky outside was just beginning to brighten with dawn, and he felt like taking on the world. Amazing what a little bit of food, some great sex, and a good night's sleep would do for a man.

He slid out of bed without disturbing Isa and went outside. Maya followed him out. The dog trotted off into the grass to relieve herself, and he headed behind the nearest tree to do the same. The scent of smoke hung heavy in the air again this morning.

That was not good news. He walked down to the stream to splash some cold water on his face. The sky glowed orange to his left, while the sun peeped through the trees to his right. For a moment, he could have sworn he was watching two sunrises.

Fucking hell.

That orange glow wasn't the sunrise. It was fire.

He lurched to his feet and ran back inside. "Isa, wake up."

She rolled over, smiling up at him through bleary eyes. "Morning."

"Sweetheart, I hate to rush you, but we've got to go."

"What?" She rubbed her eyes.

"The fire's gotten closer, much closer. We can't stay here."

"Oh." She sat up in bed, the blanket pooling

around her waist to reveal her breasts.

And as much as he wanted to enjoy the view, he'd been overtaken with an urgency to get the hell out of Dodge. He leaned in to give her a quick kiss, then started gathering their supplies.

Isa slid out of bed, dressed, and headed outside.

By the time she returned, he had packed their bags. He stripped the blanket and sheets off the bed, bound them into a bundle, and tied them to his duffel bag with Maya's leash. He'd also packed forks, spoons, the can opener, their one remaining match, and the can of baked beans.

"Breakfast of champions," he said, handing her a granola bar. These were their last two granola bars. They were down to a bag of potato chips and a can of baked beans. Not ideal, but they'd make it work. They had no other choice.

"This is the closest it's been," she said, eyes wide as she bit into her granola bar.

"I know."

They finished their breakfast in silence. He doused the embers in the wood stove with water from the stream, and they headed out. The sun was just peeking over the treetops.

"I'm scared," Isa said quietly, eyeing the orange glow still visible to the west.

"We're going to be okay." He pulled her in for a quick hug.

They walked to the stream to refill their water bottles.

"If we keep going the way we've been going, we're still headed more or less away from the fire, so I think we should keep following the stream," she said, pulling herself together the way she was so good at.

He admired the hell out of her for that. "I agree."

"Okay, then." She set off, leading the way out of the valley and into the forest beyond.

He fell into step beside her. Maya trotted alongside them, occasionally darting off into the trees in pursuit of a squirrel.

"I'm so glad she's back with us," Isa said.

"I am too."

"Awfully tired of hiking, though."

"Yeah." He smiled wryly as they made their way through the woods, their pace hastened by the fire at their heels. After thinking they could stay at the cabin and wait for search and rescue, being back on the run was a brutal readjustment.

"I'm always thinking, 'just around this next bend…'" she said as they rounded a bend, revealing nothing but more forest.

"And one of these times, it's going to happen." He took her hand. "We're going to round a bend and find a road, or at least a marked hiking trail."

"And please let it be today." There was a grim determination in her features.

"Maybe we should have taken food and supplies from the shack yesterday and kept walking." The thought had been nagging at him since he'd seen the glow of flames that morning. Because while he'd been romancing Isa, the fire had been closing in on them.

"No." She shook her head briskly. "It made

111

perfect sense to stay there and give search and rescue a chance to find us. Plus, we were dead on our feet when we found that place. If we hadn't stopped to recharge, we might not have had the strength to finish this."

"You're right." He knew it, but damn, he wished that wildfire had stayed put.

"Plus, it brought Maya back to us."

Isa had set a brisk pace for them, and they maintained it for most of the morning. Around noon, they paused for a quick rest to refill their water bottles and freshen up. Maya splashed in the stream while he gathered a handful of pine nuts to give them a midday boost. Smoke still hung heavy in the air but, now that the sun was high in the sky, they couldn't see any sign of the fire itself.

Still, the memory of the orange glow they'd seen on the horizon that morning spurred them on. They each crunched on a bite of pine nuts, and then they set out again, hoping against hope that they'd find rescue around the next bend.

***

Isa had started the day refreshed and ready to take on the world, and she was ending it exhausted and terrified. The glow of flames they'd seen that morning had made their situation real in a way the smoke somehow hadn't.

A forest fire was coming.

If it caught them… It was too horrible to even think about.

"Maybe we ought to keep walking," she said

after Nate suggested they start working on a shelter. "Maybe we shouldn't stop tonight."

"I don't know, Isa." He wrapped an arm over her shoulders, looking up at the rapidly darkening sky.

"We've kept pace with the fire today, but if we stop for the night, we're giving it lots of time to catch up to us." And she'd rather be tired than burn alive.

"And if one of us falls and breaks a leg in the dark, we'll be sitting ducks."

She pointed. "Look, the moon's almost full tonight. Let's at least walk for as long as it's up."

"Fair enough," he agreed. "And if we're going to keep moving most of the night, we should fuel up." He sat on a tree stump and opened his duffel bag, pulling out the can of baked beans.

"I've never liked baked beans," she said. "Until right now."

"At least they have a lot of protein."

She nodded as she sat beside him. She opened her backpack and set out a handful of food for Maya. Only one, maybe two handfuls remained. And after they ate these beans, their only remaining food was a snack-sized bag of potato chips.

They ate quietly and quickly, then packed up and kept moving. Every bone and muscle in her body ached. Fatigue pressed over her, slowing her steps. But they had to keep walking. Their lives depended on it.

Nate seemed to be feeling the same. He walked slowly, almost gingerly, beside her, his mouth set in a grim line. Maya, on the other hand, trotted ahead, scoping the land before returning to them, over and over again.

"Do you think she ever gets tired?" Isa asked.

"Doesn't seem like it. What I wouldn't give for a fraction of her energy right now."

As night fell around them, the forest came alive with new sounds. Owls hooted, and from somewhere in the distance, a coyote howled. Isa shivered.

"Better put on our jackets," Nate said. "It's getting cold fast now."

They paused to put on their jackets, and her gaze caught on the ominous orange glow behind them, visible again now that the sun had gone down. "Oh God, Nate. I think it's closer now than it was this morning."

He followed her gaze. "Yeah. I'd say you were right to keep walking."

"What if it catches us?" Fear gripped her chest, squeezing all the air from her lungs.

"We'll cross that bridge when we get to it. Right now, we're just going to keep walking."

"We could walk right past a trail tonight and never even know," she said as they struck out again. The moon cast a silvery glow over the woods around them. Any other time, she would have been scared out of her wits to be walking deep in the Sierra Nevadas after dark, but right now, her every thought was consumed by the fire on their tails.

"That's a risk we'll have to take," Nate said.

She picked her way carefully over rocks and around trees, feeling with her hands to keep from running into anything. Even so, branches slapped at her face, scratching her cheeks and snagging in her hair. Maya stayed close, and her presence was Isa's biggest comfort. If anything scary lurked nearby, Maya would alert them.

"I'm so tired," Isa muttered as she stumbled over a rock she hadn't seen, bruising her shin.

"Me too, sweetheart. Even Maya looks like she's slowing down."

The dog walked beside them now, head down and tongue out. Isa's eyes stung with fatigue—or maybe it was just the smoke, which seemed to grow heavier all the time. As they struggled on, the moon dipped below the treetops, and the darkness around them deepened. Her shoulders ached from too many hours spent wearing a heavy backpack.

"This is where we stop and rest for a few hours," Nate said softly beside her.

"We can't stop..." she whispered.

"We have to, Isa. We can't see a damn thing without the moon, and our bodies will give out if we don't get a few hours' sleep. It can't be long until dawn. We'll just rest until then."

"Okay," she conceded.

He knelt and started testing the ground around them. It was too dark to make a shelter, and she was too tired to build one in any case. She heard the rustling of cloth.

"What are you doing?" she whispered.

"Making us a bed. Come on down."

She knelt, surprised to feel a blanket beneath her fingers. "Oh my God, I forgot you brought the bedding from the cabin with us."

"Been carrying it all damn day. Okay, let's sleep."

115

She set her backpack on the ground and crawled forward, feeling her way into the bed Nate had made for them.

"I figure we'll lie on the sheet and keep the blanket over us for warmth."

"Sounds good to me." She snuggled in beside him, relieved beyond words to be off her feet and beneath a warm blanket. "At least we don't have much food left to attract bears…"

"Yep." He rolled onto his side, wrapping an arm around her. Maya curled up in front of her, sandwiching her between warm dog and warm man.

And even though the ground was cold, hard, and lumpy beneath her, she dropped straight off to sleep, with flames dancing behind her eyelids. She woke what felt like moments later to Nate rubbing her shoulder.

"Time to get moving," he murmured in her ear.

"But…" She started to say they'd just lain down, but as she opened her eyes, she saw that dawn was already brightening the sky overhead. She groaned as she sat up. Her body felt like she'd been trampled by horses during the night. There wasn't one square inch of her that didn't hurt.

"You sleep okay?"

"Yeah." She struggled to her feet, gasping as she stared into the distance. A thick, black wall of smoke hung over the forest, and for the first time, red flames were visible, licking at the sky. "Oh God."

"I know." He started to roll up their blanket.

Maya whined, pacing anxiously around them.

Moving almost mechanically, Isa bent to feed

the dog, then walked far enough into the woods for privacy to pee. Her brain was still trying to process this new reality. The fire was closing in on them. What were they going to do?

She hurried down to the stream to refill her water bottle. Nate met her there, duffel already stowed over his shoulder. He held the bag of potato chips in his hands.

"This is all we have left. We should eat them now, I think, to give us a boost before we head out."

"Let's eat while we walk," she suggested, accepting a handful of potato chips from him.

He nodded, falling into step beside her. "We're going to make it out of here, Isa."

"I sure hope so." She resisted the urge to glance over her shoulder. The fire was there. She didn't need to see it to be reminded of it. Despite a few hours' rest, she was exhausted. Her feet ached, and she was sure she'd find new blisters if she took the time to remove her sneakers and check.

"We've made it this far." He took her hand and squeezed.

It was such a small gesture, but he'd held her hand through so much of this ordeal, and it was just so…*nice* wasn't a strong enough word. *Vital* came closer to expressing the warmth in her chest when his fingers squeezed hers. Because without him beside her, she wasn't sure how much farther she'd make it.

"I've lost track of the days," she said. At this point, it felt like she'd been lost in the forest with Nate for years.

"I think it's Friday."

Friday. Only five days. How was that even

possible?

She chewed and swallowed a potato chip. It was salt and vinegar, a flavor she usually loved. This morning, though, it burned in her mouth. So salty. So sour. She gagged as she swallowed.

"Really wish these were pancakes," she muttered.

"Or a big Denver omelet."

"My grandma made a mean omelet." She twisted her right ring finger, remembering the butterfly ring she'd lost in the lake. "Our families must be so worried." She tried not to let herself dwell on it, but her parents must be out of their minds with grief and worry by now. And her sisters...

"With any luck, we'll be calling home before the end of the day."

"But how can you say that?" Tears pricked at her eyes. "When we've walked for five days without finding a single damn trail."

"That hunting cabin couldn't have been more than a day's hike from someplace, Isa. We didn't know how to follow the trail, but this stream's taking us somewhere. I can feel it."

"I hope you're right." As she watched, a smoldering piece of ash drifted to the ground in front of her, singeing the pine needles at her feet.

CHAPTER TWELVE

NATE was trying like hell not to panic, but no matter how far or how fast he and Isa walked, the fire only seemed to draw closer. Combined with the fact they'd walked most of the night and eaten only a handful of potato chips today, he was running on pure adrenaline.

Ash fell around them from time to time, reminding them of the fiery beast on their tails.

"I'm so tired," Isa mumbled as they climbed over yet another rock. Dark smudges pooled beneath her eyes, and angry red scratches marred her face from their hike through the night.

He suspected he didn't look much better. "And hungry."

"Yeah, that too."

Neither of them suggested they stop to forage. They both knew there was no time for that.

"Around the next bend," she muttered.

"One of these times, it will be true." He kept his hand in hers, offering his support but also taking strength from the connection between them.

"Let it be this time," she said as they rounded the bend, only to find another stretch of endless forest. "Shit."

Smoke filled the sky ahead. Had the fire encircled them? Or was the wind just messing with them? A fist clenched around his gut. They were going to make it out of here alive. He refused to accept any other outcome.

They walked on, weaving their way through the forest as they followed the stream on its endless journey to…somewhere. Several times, they scrambled down steep slopes to stay alongside it. No time for detours today.

No time for anything except putting as much distance between themselves and the fire as possible. The duffel bag bounced awkwardly against his back, weighed down by the bundle of blankets. "I think we should consider lightening our load," he said finally.

She looked at him in alarm. "How do you mean?"

"These bags are slowing us down. We've barely eaten anything in the last two days. We're running on fumes, Isa. We need to do whatever we can to move as quickly as we can."

"And we don't need most of this stuff anymore anyway, right? Either we'll make it out of here soon, or…we won't." She swiped a tear from her cheek, nodding.

That small action broke him to pieces. Through all this, Isa had been a fucking rock, and to see her cry now... He tugged her up against him and kissed her. "We're making it out of here."

"I want to believe you," she whispered against his lips.

He wanted to believe himself too. They stopped and dumped out their bags, leaving most of their belongings behind. They kept their water bottles, the pocket knife, the blanket, and a few toiletries, putting everything into Isa's backpack. It was more comfortable than his duffel bag, and they would take turns carrying it.

With that done, they kept walking. As the sun began to slip down toward the treetops, Maya—who'd spent most of the day whining and pacing anxiously around them—took off into the woods, leaving them behind.

"She looks like she's making a run for it," Isa said quietly.

"She does."

"Should we follow her?"

"No. She's already gone." The dog had disappeared into the trees.

"Good for her," Isa said. "No reason for her to hang back with us slow humans. I hope she makes it."

"I do too." But the truth was, his conviction was beginning to waver. His exhaustion had reached the point where each step required a mental effort. He felt light-headed, and the heavy smoke made his eyes water.

"When we get out of here," Isa said, her voice quiet but strong, "we'll find her."

"Damn straight." He gave her hand another squeeze.

"What will you do first?" she asked, glancing in his direction.

"What?" He coughed.

"When we get out of here, what will you do first?"

"Kiss you," he answered without thinking. "And then eat a really big meal."

"I want a cheeseburger," she said. "With mustard and pickles. And lots of french fries."

His mouth watered at the thought. "That sounds like perfection."

"And then a really long, hot shower." She closed her eyes, smiling dreamily. "And then a bed."

"I would love to join you for all those things."

She gave him an amused look. "I would love that, but no offense...I need to actually sleep before I could sleep with you again."

"I've never been this tired in my whole life, but I could probably still get hard for you, Isa. You turn me completely inside out just looking at you." And it was more than just physical attraction. He loved being with her—even though they'd shared pretty much nothing but dire straits since they met. She made him laugh. Made him *feel*.

And right now she was looking at him like she wanted to jump his bones. Or maybe like she wanted to take him home to meet the family, because the look in her eyes seemed to run much deeper than attraction too.

He said nothing because he didn't want to ruin the moment, no more than he wanted to break her heart. He just kept walking, hustling them along and hoping for a miracle.

***

"Too bad my Fitbit got ruined when we had to swim out of the lake," Isa said as they walked. "Can you imagine how many steps we've walked by now?"

"So many you might have broken it." Nate smiled. His eyes were tired, and several days of stubble coated his cheeks, and he was the most handsome thing she'd ever seen.

The sun had dropped beneath the treetops, casting long shadows around them. Behind them, the fire glowed ever brighter. It was windy today. The breeze kept blowing her hair in her face and sending smoldering ash through the air around them.

Wind like that couldn't be good news. Already, they'd dodged several small brushfires. No matter how far or how fast they walked, it was closing in on them.

"Nate..." She didn't even know what to say.

"I know, sweetheart." He squeezed her hand.

The forest around them was silent except for the rustling of the wind. Not even a bird squawked overhead. All of nature's creatures seemed to have fled.

"We'll have to walk through the night again," she said.

He nodded. "Maybe we should take a few

123

minutes to gather pine nuts before it gets any darker."

"I don't know." She glanced back at the fire. Hunger was a constant ache in her stomach, but was it worth losing precious time while they foraged for a handful of food? "We might use more calories hunting for them than we'd gain in eating them."

"You might be right about that." He stopped walking, drawing her in for a kiss. "I can't imagine doing any of this without you."

"Promise you won't walk out of my life when we get home." Tears stung her eyes. Her heart pounded, and her head swam.

"Isa, you know I can't—"

"Don't give me more bullshit about loving your job." She jabbed a finger against his chest. "I love my job too. This thing between us is more than just two people stuck in a survival situation."

His arms tightened around her. "I know that."

"Then promise me that we'll see each other again after this is over. If we make it home in one piece, we owe ourselves that much. At least a date to see how we fit together in the real world."

His brown eyes locked on hers. "I promise."

"Okay." She blinked away her tears and kissed him like her life depended on it...because maybe it did. Their tongues tangled as all her fear and exhaustion ignited into pure, raw lust. Nate's cock pressed against her belly. She smiled against his lips. "You weren't lying when you said you could still get hard."

He rocked his hips against hers. "I don't think I could ever be too tired, or too hungry, or too *anything* to get hard for you, Isa. But we don't have the

124

energy—or the time—to waste fooling around right now."

"But once we're safe…"

"Count on it." He gave her another quick kiss, then took her hand, and they set out again, walking into the darkening night.

She drew in a deep breath and coughed. "Around the next bend…"

***

Nate thought he must look like one of the zombies on *The Walking Dead* right now. He staggered through the dark, feeling his way along like a blind man with Isa at his side. They fumbled and groped through the woods as they had done the night before until the moon sank below the horizon, leaving them in total darkness. Then they sank to the ground, wrapped themselves in the blanket, and slept.

He woke with a start sometime later, coughing from the smoke. The sky above was beginning to brighten, which meant it was time for them to move on. His hand rested over the hollow of Isa's stomach. She'd lost so much weight. No doubt he had too. It was Saturday now. Would they find their way out of this mess today?

"Rise and shine," he whispered into her ear, and she stirred, grumbling under her breath.

He stood, alarmed at how weak and sluggish he felt. This morning marked twenty-four hours since they'd had even a bite of food, over forty-eight since they'd had anything significant to eat. While Isa walked toward the stream, he gathered as many pinecones as he could find, using his pocket knife to pry out the pine nuts.

It wasn't much, but it was something.

"It's gotten closer," she said when she came back. "The fire looks like it's all around us." She hugged herself. "I'm scared, Nate."

"I am too." He handed her half the pine nuts, about ten each.

"Thank you." She popped them into her mouth.

He did the same, rolling up their blanket as he chewed.

"Here goes nothing," Isa said as they struck out.

Smoke rose from the trees all around them. It was hard to tell which direction it was coming from now. Since they knew there was nothing but forest behind them, they kept moving forward, following the stream and hoping it led somewhere.

But it didn't. They kept up their forward march, conversation between them becoming sparse as the day wore on. On and on they walked, as the wind whipped around them and the fire drew ever closer. From time to time, they called for Maya, but he didn't think either of them expected her to return this time. With any luck, she was already miles away from here, somewhere safe.

"I can see the flames," Isa said quietly, looking into the trees to their right.

Sure enough, orange flames flickered against the treetops. The air around them was heavy, thick with smoke. They walked faster. The wind whistled around them, but now he could also hear the crackle and pop of the flames.

"Around the next bend," Isa said as they followed a curve in the stream. She said it every time, although it was getting harder to hope civilization lay around the next bend. The forest around them seemed as remote as ever.

A hiking trail was possible, though, and it was better than nothing.

They rounded the bend, and Isa stopped short with a gasp. "Oh no."

Flames leaped through the treetops ahead.

"Shit," he muttered.

She turned to bury her face against his chest. They were surrounded by fire. This was not good. This was so incredibly bad. For the first time, he considered the fact that they might not get out of here alive. The thought of dying out here in the woods, of losing Isa…

"It's time for Plan B," she said against his chest.

"What's that?"

She lifted her head. "We have to leave the stream."

"Yeah, okay." Their chances grew even more slim once they'd left the stream that had guided them all this way, but she was right. There was no other way. And they weren't going to give up. Not yet. Not ever.

They refilled their water bottles before striking off into the woods. The terrain was more uneven here, rocky and hilly. And they were both so tired, so weak. But she still wasn't complaining, and neither was he. They adjusted their course here and there to keep heading toward the brightest patch of sky overhead, no longer caring about moving in a straight line as much as just staying away from the fire.

"I'm just—I'm tired." Isa propped her hands on her thighs, bent over and gasping for breath. Her face was alarmingly pale.

Nate was damn near tapped out himself, and he had a lot more body mass to fall back on than she did. "I'll gather a few more pine nuts. You sit and rest for a minute."

She sat without protest, which let him know how bad off she truly was. He spent the next few minutes gathering pine cones, providing them both with another mouthful of food.

Then they forged on.

"Nate." Isa gripped his arm, and her tone sent fear down his spine. "Look."

Flames glowed through the trees ahead. Close. Way too fucking close. He gripped her arm and hauled her to the left, away from the fire, but after a few minutes, they ran into it again.

"Behind us," she said, reversing direction.

The sun dipped low in the sky, marking the end of another day, but this time, it didn't leave them in darkness. All around them the forest glowed. The flames crackled and hissed as they devoured trees, drawing ever closer.

"There is no way I'm burning to death in these woods," Isa said, grim determination in her tone.

"I am right there with you on that."

Adrenaline flooded through him. They broke

into a run, headed for the darkest part of the forest ahead. He slid the backpack from his shoulders and dropped it. They ran for their lives, ducking and dodging around tree branches. His lungs burned, and his legs shook. Beside him, Isa coughed, wheezing with each breath.

On and on they raced. Flames licked at them from every direction, close enough to feel their heat on his skin.

"I can't breathe," Isa gasped, stumbling against him.

Fear knifed through him as he wrapped his arm around her waist. "I've got you, sweetheart."

He held on to her, supporting her as they forged on. His eyes caught on something up ahead, something dark glistening beneath the moon.

"Water," she whispered.

They'd run back into the stream. Or a different stream, but water nonetheless. And water didn't burn. In silent unison, they plunged into it, sloshing to the center as flames licked at their heels.

"What now?" She wrapped her arms around him, gazing wide-eyed around them.

The flames had surrounded them. The smoke was so thick, he could barely breathe. Each breath drew a hacking cough from his lungs, and tears streamed from his eyes.

"That way looks better." He motioned downstream, where the fire seemed less thick.

The water reached their knees, ice cold and moving fast. The rocks beneath it were smooth and slippery. The perfect recipe for disaster, but he didn't care. They had to keep walking. Isa clung to him, coughing and wheezing. Her body shook, whether from cold or fear, he didn't know.

"I can't—" She fell to her knees, coughing.

"It's okay."

"It's not." Her eyes were wide and glassy, her breathing ragged.

Flames reached toward them from both banks. The stream was only about five feet wide, not nearly wide enough to protect them. The heat of the fire singed his upper body while his lower legs grew numb from the water.

"C-can't breathe." She sank to her knees in the water, scooping handfuls that she poured into her mouth. Then she sat back, clutching at her chest.

The truth was, he was having trouble breathing too. Every time he inhaled, it felt like flames had invaded his lungs. Spots danced around his vision.

He sat, letting the water swirl over him. Isa crawled into his lap, wrapping her arms around his neck and clinging to him. "I think…this is it, Nate." Tears streamed over her cheeks.

"Don't say that." Desperation roared inside him. It couldn't end for them now, not like this.

"It's not…so bad," she gasped. "The smoke will get us here…not fire."

"Don't give up, Isa." The urge to run was so strong. Surely around the next bend—

"I'm not giving up…but it's out of our hands now." She tipped her face toward the sky, her breaths shallow and rapid.

The flames had walled them in. They could try to keep picking their way downstream, but it would be slow going. Still, it was better than sitting here...

"Nate"—she gripped his face, staring into his eyes—"when the plane was crashing...one of the irrational things that went through my head was that I'd die without ever having been in love." She broke off as a fresh round of coughing racked her body.

"We're not going to die." He tightened his arms around her. They needed to get up, keep walking...

"Listen to me," she gasped. "Now that's not true, because I'm falling in love with you."

"Isa—" His heart clenched painfully at her words.

"Wanted you to know," she murmured as her eyes fluttered shut, and she fell limp in his arms.

No! "Isa..." He shook her gently, but she didn't stir. Frantic, he pressed his ear to her chest. Her heart thumped steadily against his ear, and her chest still rose and fell with rasping breaths. She was alive, but for how long?

"Hang in there, sweetheart. I'm going to get us out of this." He struggled to his feet with her in his arms, but the smoke was too thick. He couldn't see, couldn't breathe. "I'm falling for you too, Isa. Don't you dare leave me now."

The noise of the fire seemed to intensify. It roared around him, punctuated by some kind of rhythmic sound, almost like static. And now he was hallucinating. Shapes moved around him, alien shapes with black hoses where their faces should be.

"Help," he gasped, clutching Isa's limp body in his arms.

131

"Over here!" a man's voice yelled, and this was no hallucination. Firefighters in full suits and face masks were sloshing through the water toward him. "Holy shit, are you the missing people from that plane crash?"

Nate nodded as he held tight to Isa, her beautiful face illuminated by the flames, so pale, so still. "Please help us."

CHAPTER THIRTEEN

ISA remembered voices shouting. Nate's face leaning over hers, an oxygen mask covering his nose and mouth. Being bumped and jostled until her bones felt like they might come apart. Lights and beeping. Pain. Lots of pain. With a gasping breath, she lurched upright. Her eyes focused on a hospital room. Nate lay slumped in the chair beside her bed, asleep.

We're safe.

Tears flooded her eyes and streamed over her cheeks.

Safe.

She was alive. Nate was alive. And they were safe. She pressed her hands over her face and sobbed, gasping and coughing through her tears.

"What's wrong, sweetheart?" Nate slid onto

the bed beside her. He lifted her hands, kissing away her tears as he straightened the oxygen tube running to her nose

"Nothing's wrong," she gasped. "Everything's right."

"Damn straight." He pressed his lips to hers.

"How?" Because she remembered being in that stream as the smoke and the flames surrounded them. She remembered passing out in Nate's arms, certain that she was dying. *I remember telling him I was falling in love with him…*

"Firefighters. Smoke jumpers, I think. They were out there on the frontlines trying to contain the fire and stumbled across us in the process."

"Wow." She sucked in a breath and blew it out. Her lungs hurt. Actually, her whole body hurt, but she didn't care. She was alive!

Nate stroked a finger across her face, his expression fierce yet tender. "Damn lucky."

They'd come so close to not making it out. Way too close…

She coughed. Her throat felt like she'd swallowed knives, and her lungs burned with each breath she took. Nate poured her some ice water from a cart beside the bed, and she took several grateful sips.

"We're safe," she whispered as the room swam before her eyes. She was so tired…

Nate set the cup down and lay down beside her. "Rest, sweetheart. Sleep."

She wanted to hold on to him and never let go. She still had so many questions… But her brain just wouldn't cooperate. She drifted off to sleep with

Nate's arms wrapped warm and tight around her. She woke to the sound of voices. Familiar voices. Her eyes snapped open.

"Isa!" Her mother grabbed her in a hug. "Oh my goodness, *mija*."

"Mami?" She blinked, still not entirely sure she wasn't dreaming.

"I've been so worried." Her mother's voice broke, and then they were both sobbing, holding on to each other for dear life.

"I still can't believe I'm safe." When she closed her eyes, she expected to see flames, smell smoke. She felt an overwhelming need to run and run and run...

"You're safe." Her mother kissed her forehead as tears streamed down her cheeks. "I never gave up hope, even when they started telling us that they didn't expect to find you alive—"

Isa clung to her mother, sobbing as all the shock and fear of her week in the woods with Nate finally caught up with her. When the flames surrounded them at the end, and she'd realized there was no way out... It was something she'd never forget, something she hoped never to experience again.

"You are a sight for sore eyes." Her father came into her line of vision, a tired smile on his face. Her sisters Valentina and Andrea stood on either side of him, their eyes red-rimmed.

"We got on the first plane out here as soon as we heard," Andrea said.

They all huddled around her, crying and hugging, and Isa was afraid to blink for fear she might

135

realize it was all a hallucination and she was still out there in the woods with the wildfire closing in on them...

"Where's Nate?" she asked, coughing as she wiped away her tears.

"Who?" Her mother's brow wrinkled.

"Nate...the guy I was with. The pilot." The man she'd fallen in love with while they fought for their lives.

"I don't know. Is he here in the hospital too?"

"He was here earlier." She squeezed her eyes shut, trying to remember. Had it been this morning? What day was it anyway? She didn't even know what hospital she was in.

"Well, we haven't seen him." Her mother reached behind her to fluff her pillow. "How are you feeling? Can I get you anything?"

She felt like she'd swallowed fire and been run over by a Mack truck. "I'm okay."

Where's Nate?

They'd made promises out there in the woods, but the truth was, she didn't really know if Nate would still be *her* Nate back here in the real world. Had he left without even saying goodbye?

"Are you hungry?" her mother asked.

Isa shook her head. She'd been hungry for a week, but now she'd lost her appetite.

***

Nate's first day back in the real world had not gone at all as expected, but with any luck, it was going to end well. Blowing out a breath, he raised his fist

136

and knocked. The door to the hotel room in front of him swung open, and he found himself facing an attractive, middle-aged woman with Isa's eyes and smile.

"You must be Mrs. Delgado," he said.

"Yes." She offered him a warm smile. "And who are you?"

"Nathaniel Peters, ma'am. I'm the pilot who spent the last week stranded with your daughter."

Mrs. Delgado's eyes brightened. "Oh, she's been looking for you all afternoon. Come on in."

He stepped inside, finding the room filled to bursting with Isa's family. Isa herself was sitting in bed, looking fresh-faced and ridiculously gorgeous in a pink T-shirt and matching pajama pants, talking to a woman who had to be her sister. As he watched, she turned her head in his direction, and her mouth fell open.

"Nate!" She leaped out of bed and was halfway across the room when her gaze dropped to the dog at his side. "Oh my God, Maya!"

"We made it," he said as she flung herself into his arms and planted a quick, chaste kiss on his lips—her whole family was watching, after all. "All three of us."

"I am so happy right now." She dropped to her knees to hug the dog. "I've been so worried about you, Maya, thinking you were still out there in that fire."

"She made it out before we did," Nate told her. "Spent last night in the shelter."

"How did you find her?" Isa stood to face him, smiling, her eyes shining with happy tears.

137

"I asked around while we were at the hospital, and they called the shelter for me. But by the time I'd gotten her, you'd already been discharged."

"I was afraid you'd left." There was something fragile in her smile.

"I promised I wouldn't." He looked her straight in the eye. Leaving had crossed his mind, though, and frankly, he was terrified to be here in her hotel room with her family, because what if things were different now that they were back in the real world? Except every time he looked at Isa, he knew they weren't.

"Is that what I think it is?" Her gaze fell to the big paper bag in his left hand.

"Burgers and fries."

"With pickles? And mustard?" Her smile grew even wider.

He nodded. "You said it's what you wanted for your first meal. I wasn't sure how many people were here, so I brought a dozen."

"Isa, we love him already," one of her sisters commented from behind them, and the whole room erupted with laughter.

And so they all gathered on the two double beds, and they ate burgers and fries. They laughed, and they shared stories. He and Isa told her family about their week in the woods, and they in turn embarrassed Isa by sharing childhood stories about her with him.

They were warm and funny and obviously loved her to pieces. He didn't know how much she'd told her family about their relationship, but they obviously knew *something*, and they seemed to have welcomed him with open arms.

When all the food had been eaten and stories shared, her mother stood from the bed. "Okay, I know you two need a few minutes alone to catch up, but *only* a few minutes." She gave Nate a meaningful look. "She needs her rest, and I'm guessing you do too."

"Yes, ma'am." He smiled at her, grateful for the opportunity.

Isa's family shuffled toward the door.

"We'll be in the adjoining room," her father said with another pointed look at Nate.

As soon as the door shut behind them, he grinned. So did she. And then she was in his arms. "I'm so happy, Nate. I keep thinking I'm going to wake up and find out we're still out there in the woods."

"This is real, sweetheart." He tightened his arms around her, tipping her face up to kiss her.

"They like you," she said, nodding her head in the direction of the door her family had just left through.

"Thank goodness for that."

"Are your parents here too?"

He shook his head. "The trip was too much for my mom, but I talked to her for about an hour on the phone this morning. I'll go visit them in the next few days."

"I'm glad. What happens next?" she asked, her eyes searching his.

"I'm flying home in the morning. I have to get things squared away with work. God knows what's gone on this week without me."

139

She nodded. "And then?"

"And then, I thought maybe I could fly down to Anaheim and take you on that date we talked about."

"Yes," she whispered against his lips. "Except the flying part."

"You'll fly," he said, kissing her, losing himself in her taste, her warmth, every sweet thing that made Isa so damn special. "Because the Isabel Delgado I fell in love with doesn't let fear boss her around."

She inhaled sharply. "Oh! But—"

"Yes, I love you, Isa." So much that his heart felt full every time he was in the same room with her. "You've turned the cynic into a believer."

"I love you too," she whispered, her eyes welling with tears. "So much that I'll even agree to the *possibility* of flying with you on that date."

"I like the sound of that. I'd better go now before your parents think we're getting it on in here." He winked at her.

Isa blushed adorably. "Okay."

"Should I leave her with you?" He gestured to Maya, passed out on the floor by the bed in a burger-induced coma.

"Yes."

He pulled Isa in for another kiss, then he walked toward the door. "I'll be in touch about our first date."

"It's not our first date!" she said laughingly, following him.

"First official date. First of many."

"Maybe even our last," Isa said with a sly

smile.

"Last?"

"Last first date." She went up on her tiptoes to give him another kiss. "Because after everything we've already survived together, I'm not planning to give you up."

EPILOGUE

As it turned out, their first date was at the big table in Isa's parents' backyard with her whole family joining them. She'd had to move back in with her parents until she could find a new apartment that allowed big dogs, because, after everything they'd been through, there was no way she could give Maya away.

As it also turned out, getting back on an airplane wasn't nearly as easy for her as Nate seemed to have hoped. So, apart from one road trip to Fresno to meet his parents, Nate had flown his new plane to Anaheim once a week or so to spend time with her.

That was great...for now. But they needed a long-term solution to their long-distance relationship, and she wasn't sure what it would be. She couldn't imagine leaving the Los Angeles area and her family behind, but sometimes love involved compromise, and her love for Nate had only grown in the months since they'd been rescued.

The doorbell rang, and she hurried to answer it.

Nate stood there in khaki slacks and a periwinkle-blue button-down shirt, looking so handsome, her heart did a little dance in her chest. *My man.* How did she get so lucky?

"You look gorgeous," he said, leaning in to kiss her. "I'm still not used to seeing you all dressed up like this."

She blushed, running her hands over the front of her dress. "Thanks. I was just thinking the same thing about you."

"Ready?" he asked.

"Yeah." He'd called earlier and asked her to pack an overnight bag, and she couldn't wait to find out where they were going.

"I've got big plans for us tonight." He threaded his fingers in hers and drew her up against him. "And, if you're willing, I'd really like to start by taking you up in my new plane."

Her throat constricted painfully. "Nate, I don't—"

"Just try. That's all I ask. At least sit inside it. If that's all you want to do today, we'll drive instead of fly, but San Diego's a two-hour drive." He lifted his eyebrows meaningfully.

San Diego. "Our fantasy date."

"It's about damn time, don't you think?"

She nodded, her throat gone dry. "Yes."

"Flying time's about forty-five minutes. We

have dinner reservations at that Italian place I was telling you about, right on the waterfront."

"Dinner, and then a romantic stroll on the beach," she said softly.

"And then to our hotel room overlooking the ocean."

"Ooh la la!" Andrea said from behind them, giving Isa a playful slap on the shoulder.

"Let's get out of here." Isa grabbed her purse and her overnight bag before her whole family barged in on them. "Bye!" she called over her shoulder to her sister.

"Have fun," Andrea replied, still grinning.

Isa followed Nate to the car. Twenty minutes later, they were walking out onto the tarmac, headed for a shiny silver deathtrap of a plane. It all felt a little *too* familiar.

"We won't be flying over any mountains today," he said, hooking an arm around her shoulders. "In fact, I plan to take us down the coastline all the way. Beautiful views."

"Mm-hmm." She swallowed hard. "Nate—"

"Just sit inside, Isa." He squeezed her hand the way he'd done so many times when they were lost in the woods together.

"Okay." She walked toward the passenger door and climbed inside, her heart fluttering like a hummingbird. "It looks just like your other plane."

"Nah." He climbed into the pilot's seat beside her. "This one's got some snazzy new features. I'd love to show them off for you."

She clutched the leather armrest, remembering the deafening silence once the engine

144

had stopped over the Sierra Nevadas. The way her life had flashed before her eyes as they prepared to crash. The boom when he'd pulled the parachute. The hard slam of the plane into the lake. Her throat closed up, and a cold sweat broke out across her body.

"Isa," Nate said quietly, giving her hand another squeeze. "The woman I fell in love with bravely faced every hardship that came our way out there in those mountains. You led the way even when things got so tough, most people would have given up. You survived crash-landing in the mountains in the middle of a forest fire. Today's flight will be boring by comparison, I promise you."

She didn't speak, couldn't speak.

"Sweetheart, you're the strongest, bravest woman I know. You can do this, but I'm also happy to drive if you're not ready."

She looked over at him, seeing the sincerity in his eyes and the love stamped all over his face. "Okay," she said finally. "Let's do it."

"You just made me a very happy man." He leaned in to give her a scorching kiss. When he lifted his head, his expression had glazed over with lust. "I've never made out in my plane before. Need to do it more often."

"Yes." She managed a smile, her heart racing now as much from desire as fear.

He was right. She could do this. It was ridiculous to let herself be ruled by an irrational fear. She'd already lived through the worst-case scenario. Now it was time to learn to enjoy something that was such a huge part of Nate's life.

She distracted herself by fantasizing about the

evening to come while he talked to Air Traffic Control and guided them out to the runway.

"Hang on, sweetheart," he said with a smile as the plane picked up speed. "It's going to be worth it. Trust me."

"I do," she whispered, clutching at his arm as they barreled down the runway. When the plane lifted into the air, her stomach dropped, and her head started to spin. "Nate!"

"You're doing great." He gave her a reassuring smile. "I'll take your hand just as soon as I get us up."

"Don't you dare take your hands off the controls," she gasped, smiling involuntarily.

"I would never endanger you, Isa."

"Did you order wine and chocolate-covered strawberries?" she asked breathlessly, trying to distract herself from the incessant flopping sensation in her stomach.

"Sure did." He grinned at her. "And a few other things."

"Other things?" She gasped as the plane banked to the left.

"I have a few surprises planned for tonight."

Something about the way he said it made her stomach clench in a totally different way. "I like surprises."

"Glad to hear it."

After a few minutes, the plane leveled out. The California coastline glistened beneath them like something out of a painting, with miniature waves rolling against an endless stretch of sand. It was beautiful. She blew out several long, slow breaths as

146

her heart rate returned to normal.

"Nothing sexier than the sight of you here in my plane," Nate said, his voice low and gruff.

She laughed. "Now you're being ridiculous."

"I'm not." He shot her a heated look. "Two of my favorite things, together again at last. Wasn't sure when I'd get to see it."

"You were right. It's not so bad now that we're up here."

"Quite a view." He nodded toward the crystalline coastline below.

"Yes." She leaned over and pressed a kiss to his cheek.

"Hell, Isa. I had this all planned out, but I can't wait." He reached into his back pocket, sliding something onto his palm. "The sight of you up here…in my plane… I can't think of a more perfect time or place."

"For what?" she asked, her pulse kicking back up because the look on his face was more intense than she'd ever seen.

He turned in his seat, and *oh my God*, he was holding a ring box! Her heart swooped, much like the plane had done when it left the runway. He opened the box to reveal a dazzling diamond ring inside. "Isabel Delgado, I had no idea how my life was going to change when I took you and Maya on that rescue flight. We got thrown in over our heads, and a lot of people might have ended up hating each other after some of the things we went through, but every challenge only brought us closer together."

Tears spilled over her eyelids.

"You convinced me to give love a second

chance, and I've never been happier. Will you make me the happiest man in the world and say you'll be my wife?"

"Yes." She flung her arms around him, knocking off his headset as she kissed him like crazy. Her elbow whacked one of the plane's controls, and it lurched beneath them. She squeaked in terror.

"No worries, sweetheart." He reached around her to steady them. Then he slid the ring onto her finger. "Fucking beautiful." He ran his thumb over her finger where his ring now sat.

"It's gorgeous. It's—*oh*." On either side of the diamond, tiny butterflies had been engraved in the gold band. Like her grandmother's ring…

"I went to see your parents, to get their blessing," Nate said. "And your mother gave me that diamond. It had been part of a necklace of your grandmother's. She thought I might like to have it for your ring."

Tears splashed down her cheeks. "It's perfect."

"I've been making some changes at Sequoia Group this month, arranging to move our office space from San Francisco to Los Angeles. We can buy a house together in Anaheim, with a big backyard for Maya."

"Yes." Yes, yes, *yes!*

"She won't have snow, but we can fly north for a vacation any time you like."

"I think—" She blew out a breath, tearing her gaze from her new ring to look into Nate's eyes. "I couldn't imagine anything better."

ACKNOWLEDGEMENTS

THANKS as always to my family for supporting me, especially when I became a hermit for about two weeks while writing this book! Thank you to my wonderful agent Sarah Younger and Natanya Wheeler at NYLA for your help with *Crash and Burn*. Thanks also to my editor, Linda Ingmanson, for making sure it shines. And to Annie Rains and Anna Shepherd for reading and critiquing for me.

This book required quite a bit of technical research. Thank you to Hope Freeman, Benjamin Paul, Rachel Velthuisen, and Brian Johns for your help with personal aircraft and especially how to crash one! Any mistakes are my own.

A big thank you to my loyal reader Gina Jones for letting me borrow her real-life Maya as the inspiration for the rescue dog Isa and Nate are transporting in *Crash and Burn*. I hope you love seeing Maya on the page!

And the biggest thank you of all to my readers and the bloggers and reviewers who've supported me along the way.

EXCERPT FROM UNLEASHED

LOVE TO THE RESCUE BOOK 1

CHAPTER 1

CARA Medlen felt the growl before she heard it, rumbling against her leg from the dog tensed at her side. She jiggled the leash to break his concentration. "Easy, Casper. You may not realize it yet, but today's your lucky day."

He looked up at her with dull eyes, one brown, one blue. A jagged scar creased his face. Ribs and hip bones jutted through his mangy white coat. And, oh boy, did he stink. Cara had yet to meet an ugly boxer, but Casper...well, he had the sort of face that made people cross to the other side of the street.

That same face grabbed at a tender spot in her heart.

"It's a blessing that Triangle Boxer Rescue can take him," the woman behind the desk, a volunteer named Helen, said. "Shelter life hasn't been good for him."

Cara nodded as she handed the signed paperwork to Helen. "I've worked with a lot of dogs like Casper. I'm sure we'll have him ready for adoption in no time."

But the warning she'd received from her homeowners' association over the summer weighed heavily on her mind: Keep her foster dogs in line or face disciplinary action by the board.

The door to the kennels opened, allowing raucous barking to spill into the lobby. Casper peered around her and fixed his gaze on the man who'd come through the door. His ears flattened, and the hair raised along his spine.

Yep, this dog was trouble all right.

Cara sidestepped to block his view. "Thanks, Helen. Happy New Year."

With a quick wave, she hustled Casper out the front door. He tucked his tail against the cold air, then raised his nose and sniffed the sweet scent of freedom. He slunk onto the brown patchy grass of the shelter's front lawn and raised his leg on a tree.

When he'd finished, she loaded him into the backseat of her little blue Mazda. She smoothed her hands over her black dress, wrinkled since the funeral by hours in the car and now covered in Casper's white fur. The ache in her chest rose up, squeezing her throat, and she shoved it back.

Later, she'd grieve. Now she needed to get Casper home.

She swung into the front seat and cranked the engine. "So, you've officially been sprung from doggy jail."

He gave her a wary look, then turned his head to stare out the window. She pulled onto High Street and took the ramp to Interstate 85, headed for her townhouse in Dogwood, a small town on the outskirts of Raleigh, North Carolina.

"But listen, no more shenanigans, okay?"

Casper cocked his head, his mismatched eyes somber.

"One of my fosters growled at my neighbor's dog, and she filed a complaint against me with the homeowners' association, so I need you to be on your best behavior."

With a dramatic sigh, he sprawled across the backseat and closed his eyes. Well, she'd take that as a yes. She'd put in a few extra hours of behavior training with him in the meantime, just to be sure. Casper slept for the next hour as Cara drove them home.

The latest Taylor Swift single strummed happily from inside her purse, and she shoved a hand inside to grab her cell phone. Merry Atwater's name showed on the display. "Hey, Merry."

"Hey. Just wanted to see how you're holding up," Merry said. "I've been thinking about you all day."

Cara tightened her grip on the steering wheel, blinking away the image of Gina's pale face inside the casket. "I'm okay, or I will be."

"Oh, sweetie, I'm so sorry. Let me know if there's anything I can do. Are you still planning to go out tonight?"

"Yeah, I'll be there, just maybe late. Casper and I have some acquainting to do."

"How is he?" Merry shifted into her professional voice. As the founder of Triangle Boxer Rescue, she had a vested interest in every dog they saved. Cara had no idea where she found the time to run a rescue on top of her day job as a pediatric nurse, but Merry somehow managed to juggle the two.

"Well, he's only growled twice so far." Cara

3

glanced over her shoulder with a smile. Casper watched, his head on his front paws.

"What happened? The shelter didn't mention aggression."

Cara flipped on her blinker and exited the highway onto Fullers Church Road. "I think he's just stressed out. I'm not too worried about it. What time should I meet you at Red Heels?"

"Why don't I come over to your place and we can get ready together? I'll help you get Casper settled, and we can talk."

"Sounds great, Mer, thanks."

"You bet. See you around seven."

Cara shoved the phone back into her purse. Truthfully, the last thing she wanted to do tonight was go to a New Year's Eve party, but she refused to sit home and feel sorry for herself. She'd go, and she'd even have fun, dammit.

It was what Gina would have wanted.

She pulled into the parking lot of Crestwood Gardens, her townhouse community, and guided her Mazda into its assigned spot, right next to her sexy next-door neighbor's shiny black Jeep Grand Cherokee. The man in question stood in his front yard, deep in conversation with a perky brunette in tight jeans and a low-cut sweater.

Cara felt a twinge of something like jealousy, which was ridiculous because she didn't even know his name. And she'd prefer to keep it that way. She shut off the engine and hurried to fetch Casper from the backseat. "Welcome home, dude."

He hopped down, tail tucked. It had been a long and difficult day for both of them. Time to get settled in and relax for a while.

One of her neighbors—Chuck Something-or-other—passed with a nod as Cara headed toward her townhouse. She offered a polite smile, her attention focused on Casper. The dog looked up at the older man. Their eyes met. The hair along Casper's spine raised, and he released a low, guttural growl that sent Chuck scrambling into the parking lot.

Cara swore under her breath as she shoved the key into the lock and pushed open her front door.

So much for making a good first impression on the neighbors.

RISKING IT ALL BOOK 1

CHAPTER 1

CARLY Taylor crouched behind the display case, peeking out between the blueberry muffins and the orange-cranberry scones. A man stood just inside the door, baseball cap pulled low, talking on his phone. He'd never come into A Piece of Cake Bakery before. And it was probably just her imagination playing tricks on her, but she could swear it was Sam Weiss. As in, one of the hottest rock stars in America.

Carly peeked at him again from behind the scones, then leaned over to pick up the napkin she'd pretended to drop to give herself an excuse to snoop. Sam Weiss probably lived in Hollywood. There was no way he'd be standing here—sans entourage—in the doorway of her little bakery in Haven, North Carolina, a town in the Smoky Mountains so small that it barely registered as a blip on the map.

Nope.

She was daydreaming, as usual. She'd listened to Sam's latest album, *Renegade*, this morning while she baked, and now she was imagining him here in her shop.

"What are you doing down there, Carly?"

Carly looked up to see her grandma, Marlene, peering at her over the glass countertop. "I, ah, dropped something."

"Lost in your thoughts again?" her grandmother asked with a wide smile.

"Something like that." Carly climbed to her feet, clutching the dropped napkin.

Her grandmother's friend Dixie stood beside her, her blue eyes twinkling mischievously. "Daydreaming about that handsome young man over by the door, I bet."

Carly resisted the urge to glance in his direction but felt herself grinning anyway. "I have no idea what you're talking about."

"Well, we're on our way out," her grandmother said. "Aqua aerobics to work off those muffins."

"Worth every calorie," Dixie added.

The two women waved as they headed for the door, walking past the mystery hottie as they left. Carly's grandma had created this bakery and run it happily for over twenty years. She'd retired six months ago, handing over the reins to Carly.

But owning A Piece of Cake had been anything but a piece of cake for Carly so far. Profits were down, *way* down. She needed to get her head out of the clouds—and her mind off certain rock star look-alikes—before she ran her grandmother's pride and joy straight into the ground.

With a heavy sigh, she tossed the napkin she still held into the trash.

"Hi, Carly."

She turned to find her friend Emma Rush on the other side of the counter. "Hey, Emma."

"I'm headed to a job site, and I need one of

2

your cinnamon buns to fuel me." Emma gazed longingly at the row of pastries.

Carly smiled. "And a coffee to go?"

Emma nodded. She came in about once a week for a cinnamon bun and a coffee before work.

Carly plucked a bun and slid it into one of her pastry bags. "Did you see that guy by the door when you came in?"

Emma glanced over her shoulder. "What guy?"

Carly followed her gaze. The faux rocker in the baseball cap was nowhere to be seen. She shook her head. "He must have left. He was hot, looked kind of like Sam Weiss."

Emma gave her an amused look. "Well, if he comes in, you should feed him one of your cinnamon buns. I bet he'd ask for your number."

Carly felt her cheeks flush as she filled Emma's coffee cup and pressed the lid into place. "Doubtful."

"You never know." Emma paid for her order, and with a wave, she headed for the door.

Carly glanced at her watch. Talia had called in sick today, which meant she was on her own for the day. The weather report was calling for freezing rain later so maybe she'd close early. At any rate—

"What do you recommend?"

She looked up and into the blue eyes of Sam Weiss—or his noncelebrity twin. Look-alike or not, he was ridiculously hot, and she was a dork because her cheeks were burning. He wore a leather jacket over a black T-shirt and dark-washed jeans. But his eyes…wow. He still wore the baseball cap pulled low, with a sinful amount of stubble on his cheeks that all screamed *Rock God.*

"If you have a sweet tooth, you should, um, try a cinnamon bun. They're my specialty."

He leaned in, resting his elbows on the counter. "I do have a sweet tooth, especially for a pretty woman who bakes. This your place?"

That voice. Sweet Jesus. It was smooth as caramel with just a hint of a Southern twang, and she'd know it anywhere. *Sam Weiss is in my shop! And did he just hit on me?*

"Yes." She cleared her throat because why did she suddenly sound like Minnie Mouse? "Yes, this is my shop."

A slow smile curved his lips. "A pretty woman who bakes *and* owns her own business. I like you already."

"Thanks." She really shouldn't keep staring, but whoa, her brain was short-circuiting because...Sam Weiss. In her shop. Looking like sex on a stick, and he smelled pretty awesome, too, like some kind of expensive cologne. *Yum.*

"I'll try one of your cinnamon buns…" He paused, glancing down for the name tag she never wore since everyone in town already knew her name.

"Carly," she said, still sounding a bit like she'd inhaled helium.

"Carly." He met her gaze again, and the sound of her name on his lips made her knees wobble. "And a coffee, black."

"You got it," she said with a smile that felt weird on her face, and God, why was she being such an idiot? "For here?"

4

He nodded, watching her intently as if he'd figured out by all her bumbling dorkiness that she'd recognized him because, really, how could he not? At least he looked amused instead of annoyed.

She dished up a cinnamon bun and a cup of coffee without dropping anything or making a further fool of herself, and he paid in cash—denying her the thrill of seeing what name might be on his credit card. He probably went by some cool alter ego when he traveled anyway.

"Thanks, Carly," he said in that butter-soft voice that made her feel all hot and fluttery inside. Then he leaned in, winked, and pressed a finger to his lips, making a silent, *Sh*.

And *oh my God*, he knew she knew. Which meant it was definitely him. And she grinned like an idiot while he walked to a table in the back and sat, long legs stretched in front of him. A muffled beep from the direction of the kitchen told her she'd forgotten to take the last batch of butterscotch pecan sandies out of the oven.

So much for keeping her mind on business this morning. But at this exact moment—her eyes still on Sam Weiss—she didn't care. Not even a little bit.

ABOUT THE AUTHOR

RACHEL LACEY is a contemporary romance author and semi-reformed travel junkie. She's been climbed by a monkey on a mountain in Japan, gone scuba diving on the Great Barrier Reef, and camped out overnight in New York City for a chance to be an extra in a movie. These days, the majority of her adventures take place on the pages of the books she writes. She lives in warm and sunny North Carolina with her husband, son, and a variety of rescue pets.

Rachel loves to keep in touch with her readers! You can find her at:
RachelLacey.com
Twitter @rachelslacey
Facebook.com/RachelLaceyAuthor

1927

77012563R10103

Made in the USA
Columbia, SC
17 September 2017